ADVANCED

VEDIC

MATHEMATICS

Rajesh Kumar Thakur is a mathematics teacher by profession and also a popular author. He has been the Honorary Secretary and Chairman of the Award Selection Committee of All India Ramanujan Maths Club (AIRMC) since 2012. Widely published, with more than fifty-seven books, sixty-seven e-books, and 350 blogs to his credit, Thakur is a regular columnist with over 500 published articles in various well-known newspapers and magazines including *Amar Ujala*, *Prabhat Khabar* and *Navbharat Times*. A number lover, Thakur is the recipient of several awards including the National Best Teacher Award (2010), the Arvind Pandey Yuva Lekhan Award (2015), the Math Genius Award (2017) and the Global Teacher Award (2018). He lives in Delhi, India. You can contact him at rkthakur1974@gmail.com. His Twitter handle is @R_K_THAKUR.

ADVANCED

VEDIC

MATHEMATICS

RAJESH KUMAR THAKUR

RUPA

Published by
Rupa Publications India Pvt. Ltd 2019
7/16, Ansari Road, Daryaganj
New Delhi 110002

Sales centres:

Allahabad Bengaluru Chennai
Hyderabad Jaipur Kathmandu
Kolkata Mumbai

ISBN: 978-93-5333-606-6

First impression 2019

10 9 8 7 6 5 4 3 2 1

Dedicated to Sonika Vats

Contents

Introduction

Vedic Mathematics is becoming popular day by day. In the cutthroat competition that we see in the field of mathematics today, the aspirant wants to do better and better in his/her examination, and speed and accuracy play a vital role in that. It is indeed true that the 16 sutras have not gained much popularity, and only 3 or 4 sutras have become popular. There is a great deal of competition in the market to prove each book better than the other. The numerous techniques and their attractive names can be seen everywhere, and in such a race, the essence of Vedic Mathematics is left behind. These days, most of the books available on Vedic Mathematics in the market deal with the fundamental operations of mathematics, and some algebraic concepts. Higher algebra and other branches of mathematics have been completely ignored, and most people think that Vedic Mathematics enables you to do fast multiplication and find the squares and square roots, cubes and cube roots. But the truth is that it does so much more. Vedic Mathematics is equally effective in dealing with higher algebra, some trigonometry, basic calculus, basic co-ordinate geometry etc.

I have tried to incorporate the stronger side of Vedic Mathematics, and have tried to focus on some other sutras that are not very popular. The basic use of Vedic Mathematics is fast calculation, and you can observe this fact throughout this book. Be it calculus or two-dimensional geometry or algebra, you will definitely be able to do calculations much faster than by way of traditional mathematics taught in the classroom.

The language of the book is simple and self-explanatory. You will not require a tutor or coach to teach you the higher concepts of Vedic Mathematics, as the examples are explained in a manner that will surely help you grasp the difficult concepts easily.

I have tried to explain some fundamental concepts of Vedic Mathematics while elaborating the tougher concepts in detail. For the sake of the reader, I have divided this book into two parts. In the first part, I have provided a brief note that will help you understand the importance of Vedic Mathematics and the reason why it is so popular. In the second part, you can enjoy the advanced concepts of mathematics explained in lucid language.

I hope the very effort of writing Advanced Vedic Mathematics will be highly acknowledged by my readers. The first book, *The Essentials of Vedic Mathematics* published by Rupa Publications, will introduce you to the world of Vedic Mathematics. In this book, you will develop your concepts of Vedic Mathematics further. So, enjoy reading about the ancient techniques and explore the new dimensions of mathematics.

While writing this book, I was struggling through the worst phase of my life and I can't forget to acknowledge a Ms Sonika Vats, who stood like a pillar in my difficult days and kept motivating me. I am also indebted to all my well-wishers, friends and relatives, who are constant sources of inspiration for me. I would acknowledge the help of Mr V.G. Unkalkar sir who, through our mutual friend, Mr Gaurav Tekriwal, helped me write this book. I am also thankful to the entire team of Rupa Publications, especially the editor, Yamini ji, for her firm belief in me and accepting this book despite the fact that my submission of the manuscript was delayed by almost eight months.

Finally, I would like to add that I will eagerly wait for the valuable comments of my avid readers who have always appreciated my books published by Rupa, as their comments and suggestions mean a lot to me.

Vedic Sutras

- Ekadhikena Purvena (एकाधिकेन पूर्वेण)—By one more than the previous one
- Nikhilam Navatascaramam Dasatah (निखिलम् नवतश्चरमं दशत:)—All from nine and last from ten
- Urdhva Tiryagbhyam (उर्ध्वतिर्यग्भ्याम्)—Vertically and crosswise
- Paravartya Yojayet (परावर्त्योजयेत्)—Transpose and apply
- Sunyam Samasamuccaye (शून्यं साम्य समुच्चये)—The summation is equal to zero
- Anurupye Sunyamanyat (आनुरूप्ये शून्यमन्यत्)—If one is in ratio, the other one is zero
- Sankalana–Vyavakalanabhyam (संकलन–व्यवकलनाभ्याम्)—By addition and subtraction
- Puranapuranabhyam (पूरणापूरणाभ्याम्)—By completion and non-completion
- Calana–Kalanabhyam (चलनकलनाभ्याम्)—Sequential motion
- Yavadunam (यावदूनम्)—The deficiency
- Vyastisamastih (व्यष्टि समष्टि)—Whole as one and one as whole
- Sesanyankena Caramena (शेषाण्यंकेन चरमेण)—Remainder by last digit
- Sopantyadvayamantyam (सोपान्त्य द्वयमन्त्यम्)—Ultimate and twice the penultimate
- Ekanyunena Purvena (एकन्यूनेन पूर्वेण)—By one less than the previous one

- Gunitasamuccayah (गुणित समुच्चयः)—The whole product is the same
- Gunakasamuccayah (गुणक समुच्चयः)—Collectivity of multipliers

Vedic Sub–sutras

- Anurupyena (आनुरूप्येण)—Proportionately
- Sisyate Sesasamjnah (शिष्यते शेषसंज्ञ)—Knowing remainder from remainder
- Adyamadyenantya–mantyena (आद्यमाद्येनान्त्यमन्त्येन)—First by first and last by last
- Kevalaih Saptakam Gunyat (केवलैः सप्तकं गुण्यात)—Only multiple of seven
- Vestanam (वेष्टनम्)—Osculation
- Yavadunam–Tavadunam (यावदूनम तावदूनम)—Whatever be the deficiency, lessen it further
- Yavadunam Tavadunikrtya Varganaca Yojayet (यावदूनम तावदूनम कृत्य वर्ग च योजयेत्)—Whatever the extent of its deficiency, lessen it further to that extent and set up the square of the deficiency
- Antyayotdasakepi (अन्त्ययोर्दशकेऽपि)—When the sum of the last digits is ten
- Antyayoreva (अन्त्ययोरेव)—Only the last term
- Samuccayagunitah (सामुच्चय गुणितः)—Sum of the coefficients in the product
- Lopanasthapanabhyam (लोपस्थापनाभ्याम्)—By elimination and retention
- Vilokanam (विलोकनम्)—The product of the sum of the coefficient
- Gunitasamuccayah Samuccaya gunitah (गुणित समुच्चयः समुच्चयगुणितः)—The product of the sum of the coefficients

in the factor is equal to the sum of the coefficients in the product

- Dwandwayogah (द्वंद्व योग)—Duplex combination
- Shuddah (शुद्ध:)—Dot
- Dhwajankam (ध्वजांकं)—Flag digit

PART I

1

Multiplication

Introduction

Vedic Mathematics is popular because of its use of multiplication techniques. Most people tend to know about Vedic Mathematics because of what is being taught in schools, institutions or by private coaching centres. However, they only focus on two or three techniques of Vedic Mathematics and judge its importance on the basis of just these few concepts. It is highly significant that students who appear for examinations for banking, railways, management etc. prepare for these exams by learning the innovative and quick techniques of Vedic Mathematics.

There are around 10 sutras available in Vedic Mathematics that reduce calculation time to almost one–tenth of that of the traditional methods. Here, we shall focus on 4 sutras only, in order to give you a glimpse of the aspects of Vedic Mathematics that have made it the world's fastest technique of calculation. If you want to read about them in detail, then you must read my book, *The Essentials of Vedic Mathematics*, where you will find all the 10 sutras as well as three chapters on multiplication.

Vedic Sutras

1. **Nikhilam Navatascaramam Dasatah:** The literal meaning is '**all from 9 and the last from 10**'. This means, start from the left-most digit, subtract all the digits from 9 and the last digit from 10. **This is a base method which works better when a number is close to base 10 or a multiple of 10.**

2. **Anurupyena:** This Vedic sub-sutra literally means '**proportionality**'. This sub-sutra is applicable when either the multiplicand or the multiplier is sufficiently far away from the powers of base 10. (100, 1000, 10,000 and so on are powers of base 10, but if the base is near 20, 30, 250, 500, 750, and so on, then this sutra will be applicable.)

3. **Ekanyunena Purvena:** It literally means '**one less than the previous**'. This sutra has limited application. It is used for multiplication wherein the multiplier digits consist entirely of 9s.

4. **Urdhva Tiryagbhyam:** It is a general formula applicable to all cases of multiplication. It is a process of vertical and crosswise multiplication. This method has been further simplified and dealt with using the dot and cross method in this book.

VEDIC MULTIPLICATION

Nikhilam Navatascaramam Dasatah

This sutra works better when numbers to be multiplied are very close to the base. The base should be in the form of 10^n, where n is a natural number.

Rule:

- Write the two numbers to be multiplied one above the other on the right side of your notebook's page.
- Write the deviation of the multiplicand and the multiplier from the base and place them on the right of the digits to be multiplied.
- The final result will have two parts.
  a) The left side of the answer will be obtained by cross operation of two numbers written diagonally.
  b) The right side of the answer will be obtained by multiplying the deviations.
- The number of digits on the right hand side of the separator will be equal to the number of zeros in the base number. In simple words, if the base is 100, the right hand side will have two digits, and if the base is 1,000, the right hand side will have three digits.
- In case there is a lesser number of digits on the right hand side of the separator, accommodate as many zeros before the right hand side as are required so that the total number of digits in that part is equal to the number of zeros in the base.

Base	Number of digits on the right side of the vertical line	
10	1	0
100	2	00
1000	3	000
10000	4	0000
100000	5	00000
1000000	6	000000
10000000	7	0000000

Let us see a few examples to understand the methodology of the above Vedic Sutra.

Case 1: When both the numbers are below the base

Example 1: Multiply 8 by 9.

Solution:

a) Write the multiplicand and the multiplier as shown here.

$$8$$
$$\times\ 9$$

b) Both the numbers are close to the base 10, so take Base = 10.

Deviation of 8 = 8 – 10 = – 2

Deviation of 9 = 9 – 10 = – 1

c) Write the deviations on the right side of the numbers to be multiplied.

$$8 - 2$$
$$\times\ 9 - 1$$

d) Write the left hand digit by cross operation of any of the two diagonals. Here both of them give us the same answer, as 8 – 1 = 7 and 9 – 2 = 7.

e) The right hand digit will be the multiplication of the deviations. The product of the deviations is (– 2) × (– 1) = 2.

$$8 - 2$$
$$\times\ 9 - 1$$
$$\overline{\ \ 7\ |\ 2\ }$$

= 72

Example 2: Multiply 95 by 91.

Solution:

a) Write the multiplicand and the multiplier as shown here.

$$95$$
$$\times\ 91$$

b) Both the numbers are close to the base 100, so take Base = 100.
Deviation of 95 = 95 − 100 = − 5
Deviation of 91 = 91 − 100 = − 9

c) Write the deviations on the right side of the numbers to be multiplied.

$$95 - 5$$
$$\times\ 91 - 9$$

d) Write the left hand part of the answer (numbers to the left of the separator) by cross operation of any of the two diagonals. Here 95 − 9 = 86 and 91 − 5 = 86. This is written down as the left hand part of the answer.

$$\begin{array}{r} 95 \quad 5 \\ \times\ 91 \quad 9 \\ \hline 86 \end{array}$$

e) The right hand part of the answer (numbers to the right of the separator) will be the multiplication of the deviations. (− 9) × (− 5) = 45

$$\begin{array}{r} 95 \ - \ 5 \\ \times\ 91 \ - \ 9 \\ \hline 86\ |\ 45 \end{array}$$

= 8645

Case 2: When both the numbers are above the base

Example 1: Multiply 14 by 12.

Solution:

   a) Write the multiplicand and the multiplier as shown here.

$$14$$
$$\times\ 12$$

   b) Both the numbers are close to the base 10, so take Base = 10.
Deviation of 14 = 14 − 10 = 4
Deviation of 12 = 12 − 10 = 2

   c) Write the deviations on the right side of the numbers to be multiplied.

$$14 +\ 4$$
$$\times\ 12 +\ 2$$

   d) Write the left hand part of the answer by cross operation of any of the two diagonals. Like the previous example, both give us the same answer.

$$14 +\ 4$$
$$\times\ 12 +\ 2$$
$$\overline{16}$$

   e) The right hand part of the answer will be the multiplication of the deviations. 4 × 2 = 8

$$14 +\ 4$$
$$\times\ 12 +\ 2$$
$$\overline{16\ |\ 8}$$

   = 168.

Example 2: Multiply 108 by 109.

Solution:

a) Write the multiplicand and the multiplier as shown here.

$$108$$
$$\times \ 109$$

b) Both the numbers are close to the base 100, so take Base = 100.
Deviation of 108 = 108 − 100 = − 8
Deviation of 109 = 109 − 100 = − 9

c) Write the deviations on the right side of the numbers to be multiplied.

$$108 + \ \ 8$$
$$\times \ 109 + \ \ 9$$

d) Write the left hand part of the answer by cross operation of any of the two diagonals.

$$108 + 8$$
$$\times 109 + 9$$
$$\overline{117 \ |}$$

e) The right hand part of the answer will be the multiplication of the deviations.

$$108 + 8$$
$$\times 109 + 9$$
$$\overline{117 \ | \ 72}$$

= 11772.

Case 3: When one number is more than the base and another is less than the base

Example 1: Multiply 12 by 8.

Solution: Write the multiplicand and the multiplier as shown here.

$$12$$
$$\times\ 8$$

a) Both the numbers are close to the base 10, so take Base = 10.

Deviation of 12 = 12 – 10 = + 2
Deviation of 8 = 8 – 10 = – 2

b) Write the deviations on the right side of the numbers to be multiplied.

$$12 +\ 2$$
$$\times\ 8 -\ 2$$

c) Write the left hand part of the answer by cross operation of any of the two diagonals. Both will give us the same answer. 12 – 2 = 10 and 8 + 2 = 10.

$$
\begin{array}{r}
12 + 2 \\
\times\ 8\ \ \ 2 \\
\hline
10\ |
\end{array}
$$

d) The right hand part of the answer will be the multiplication of the deviations. The product of (+ 2) × (– 2) = – 4 is written on the right side.

$$
\begin{array}{r}
12 +\ 2 \\
\times\ 8 -\ 2 \\
\hline
10\ |\ -4
\end{array}
$$

f) When the right hand digit has a minus sign, use the Nikhilam formula, which states, 'all from 9 and the last from 10'. This means, start from the left-most digit, subtract all the digits from 9 and the last digit from 10. If there is a negative sign on the right side of the separator, subtract 1 from the left side, and the right side will be subtracted from the base. Here base is 10. Subtract the right hand digit (− 4) from 10. The left hand part will get diminished by 1, i.e. 10 − 1 = 9

$$\begin{array}{r} 12 + 2 \\ \times\ 8 - 2 \\ \hline 10\ |\ -4 \\ =\ 9\ |\ 10 - 4 \\ =\ 9\ |\ 6 \end{array}$$

= 96

Example 2: Multiply 122 by 98.

Solution:

a) Write the multiplicand and the multiplier as shown here.

$$\begin{array}{r} 122 \\ \times\ 98 \\ \hline \end{array}$$

b) Both the numbers are close to the base 100, so take Base = 100.
Deviation of 122 = 122 − 100 = + 22
Deviation of 98 = 98 − 100 = − 2

c) Write the deviations on the right side of the numbers to be multiplied.

$$\begin{array}{r} 122 + 22 \\ \times\ 98 - \ 2 \\ \hline \end{array}$$

d) Write the left hand part of the answer by cross operation of any of the two diagonals.

$$\begin{array}{r} 122\quad +\ 22 \\ \times\ 98\quad -\ 2 \\ \hline 120\ | \end{array}$$

e) The right hand part of the answer will be the multiplication of the deviations.

$$122 + \widehat{22}$$
$$\times\ 98 - \widehat{2}$$
$$\overline{120\ |\ -44}$$

f) When there is a minus sign before the right hand part of the answer, use the Nikhilam formula. Here the right side of the separator has – 44, which is negative, so the left part, i.e. 119, will get diminished by 1 and the right side will be subtracted from the base 100. Subtract – 44 from 100. On the left side, 120 will get diminished by 1. i.e. 120 – 1 = 119.

$$122 + 22$$
$$\times\ 98 - 2$$
$$\overline{119\ |\ 100 - 44}$$
$$= 119\ |\ 56$$

$= 11956$

Case 4: Adjustment of right side digit of the product

In all the above three cases we have seen that the number on the right side is same as the number of zeros in the base. Now there arise two new situations. Let's have a look.

a) When the number of digits on the right hand side is more than the permissible limit.

b) When the number of digits on the right hand side is less than the permissible limit.

Subcase a: When the number of digits on the right hand side is more than the permissible limit.

Example: Multiply 18 by 16.

Solution:

a) Write the multiplicand and multiplier as shown here.

$$16$$
$$\times\ 18$$

b) Both the numbers are closer to the base 10, so take Base = 10.

Deviation of 16 = 16 − 10 = + 6

Deviation of 18 = 18 − 10 = + 8

c) Write the deviation at the right side along with the number to be multiplied.

$$16 +\ \ 6$$
$$\times\ 18 +\ \ 8$$

d) Write the left hand digit by cross operation of any of the two diagonals.

$$16 +\ 6$$
$$\times\ 18 +\ 8$$
$$24$$

e) The right hand digit will be the multiplication of the deviation.

$$16 +\ 6$$
$$\times\ 18 +\ 8$$
$$24\ |\ 48$$

Here, the number of digits on the right hand side is two, which is more than the permissible number of digits on the right hand side (See Table 1). The number of permissible digits on the right hand side should be in accordance with the base number. Since the base is 10, the number placed on the right side should be of one digit. In such a case, we transfer the extreme left digit of the right hand side to the left hand side and add them.

$$
\begin{array}{r}
16 + 6 \\
\times\ 18 + 8 \\
\hline
24\ |\ 48 \\
\end{array}
$$

$$= 288$$

Subcase b: When the number of digits on the right hand side is less than the permissible limit.

Example: Multiply 96 by 98.

Solution:

a) Write the multiplicand and multiplier as shown here.

$$
\begin{array}{r}
96 \\
\times\ 98 \\
\hline
\end{array}
$$

b) Both the numbers are closer to the base 100, so take Base = 100.
Deviation of 96 = 96 – 100 = – 4
Deviation of 98 = 98 – 100 = – 2

c) Write the deviation at the right side along with the number to be multiplied.

$$
\begin{array}{r}
96 - 4 \\
\times\ 98 - 2 \\
\hline
\end{array}
$$

d) Write the left hand digit by cross operation of any of the two diagonals.

$$
\begin{array}{r}
96 - 4 \\
\times\ 98 - 2 \\
\hline
94\ | \\
\end{array}
$$

e) The right hand digit will be the multiplication of the deviation.

$$\begin{array}{r} 96 - \textcircled{4} \\ \times\ 98 - \textcircled{2} \\ \hline 94\ |\ 8 \end{array}$$

Since the base is 100, the number placed at the right side should consist of two digits. But there is a single digit on the right hand side of the separator. In such a case, we place a zero on the left of the digit on the extreme right hand side so that the total number of digits on the right hand side is equal to the permissible number of digits. See Table 1 for better understanding.

$$\begin{array}{r} 96\ -\ 4 \\ 98\ -\ 2 \\ \hline 94\ |\ 08 \end{array}$$

Anurupyena Sutra

The word Anurupyena simply means **'proportionately'**. This method is applicable only when the multiplicand and multipliers are not exactly 10, 100, 1000 and so on...but 50, 500, 5000... or 20, 30, 40...200, 300, 400... etc.

Subcase a: When the left hand figure is completely divisible by the divisor of the working base.

Example 1: Multiply 48 by 42.

Solution: Here both the numbers are closer to 50. Now it's your choice how you would like to write 50 in multiples of 10.

$$\begin{aligned} 50 &= 100\ /\ 2 \\ &= 10 \times 5 \end{aligned}$$

In case you are taking 50 = 100/2, divide the left side of your result by 2. On the other hand, for 50 = 10 × 5, multiply the left side by 5.

Here is the example.

Working base = 100/2 = 50

Deviation of 48 from the working base = 48 – 50 = – 2

Deviation of 42 from the working base = 42 – 50 = – 8

$$48 - 2$$
$$\times\ 42 - 8$$

The working procedure is almost the same, except for the fact that the left hand side number will be divided by 2, as our working base is half of the theoretical base. As far as the right hand number is concerned, it will remain unaffected.

$$48 \qquad -2$$
$$\times 42 \qquad -8$$
$$\overline{40\ |\ 16}$$
$$= 1/2 \times 40\ |\ 16$$
$$= 2016$$

Now consider the base 50 = 10 × 5

$$48 \qquad -2$$
$$\times 42 \qquad -8$$
$$\overline{40\ |\ 16}$$
$$= 40 \times 5\ |\ 16$$
$$= 200\ |\ 16$$
$$= 2016$$

Example 2: Multiply 494 by 488.

Solution:

Theoretical Base = 1000

Working Base = 500 = 1000/2

Deviation of 494 from the working base = 494 − 500 = − 6

Deviation of 42 from the working base = 488 − 500 = − 12

Do the operation as described in the Nikhilam method, with a slight difference—the left hand figure will be divided by 2 as our working base is half of the theoretical base.

```
  494  ⟍  ⤏ − 6  ↑⟋⟍
× 488  ⟋  ⤴ − 12  |⟋
     482 | 72
```

Since the theoretical base is 1000, the number of digits on the right hand side will be three, therefore write a zero before 72.

```
  494  ⟍  ⤏ − 6  ↑⟋⟍
× 488  ⟋  ⤴ − 12  |⟋
     482 | 072
```

Now, divide the left hand side by 2.

```
  494  ⟍  ⤏ − 6  ↑⟋⟍
× 488  ⟋  ⤴ − 12  |⟋
```

2) 482 | 072   [Divide 482 by 2.]

= 241 | 072

= 241072

Subcase b: When the left hand figure, on division by the divisor of the working base, gives a fractional quotient

Example: Multiply 48 by 47.

Solution:

Working base = 50 = (100 | 2)

Step 1: Write the deviation (– 2) and (– 1) against the numbers 48 and 49, taken from the working base.

48 – 50 = – 2 and 47 – 50 = – 3

$$48 - 2$$
$$\underline{\times\ 47 - 3}$$

Step 2: Do the required operation by taking any diagonal and writing the result on the left side of the vertical line. Multiply the right hand numbers vertically.

$$45 \mid 06$$

Step 3: Divide the left hand figure by 2. Here, 47, on dividing by 2, give us a fractional quotient. i.e. 23½.

Step 4: The fractional part ½ (i.e. ½ of the theoretical base 100 = 50) is taken over to the right hand side.

2) 45 | 02
= 22½ | 02
= 22 | 50 + 2
= 2252

Subcase c: When the right hand vertical product is negative

Example: Multiply 52 by 48.
Solution: Working base = 50 = (100/2)

As discussed earlier, the excess or the deficiency from the working base is written against the number.

$52 = 50 + 2$ and $48 = 50 - 2$

$$52 + 2$$
$$\times\ 48 - 2$$

Step 1: Perform the desired operation diagonally and vertically.

$$52 \quad\quad + 2$$
$$\times\ 48 \quad\quad - 2$$
$$\overline{\quad\quad 50\ |\ -04\quad}$$

Step 2: Divide the left hand number by 2. Here 2 is the divisor of the theoretical base.

$$52 + 2$$
$$\times\ 48 - 2$$
$$2)\ \overline{\ 50\ |\ -04\ }$$
$$=\ 25\ |\ -04$$
$$25 - 1\ |\ 100 - 04$$
$$=\ 2496$$

When the right hand figure is negative, the **Nikhilam Navatas caramam dasatah** formula will be used. This simply directs us to subtract 1 from the left hand number and to subtract the right hand number from the theoretical base.

Ekanyuena Purvena

This method is the beauty of Vedic Mathematics. In most of the coaching institutes offering Vedic Mathematics classes, you will find such multiplications on their pamphlets. This sutra works under three conditions.

1) When the number of digits in the multiplicand and the number of 9s in multiplier are the same
2) When the number of 9s in the multiplier are more than the number of digits in the multiplicand
3) When there are lesser number of 9s in the multiplier than the number of digits in the multiplicand

Now let us take each case one by one

Case 1: When the number of digits in the multiplicand and the number of 9s in the multiplier are the same

Rule:

*   Subtract 1 from the multiplicand and write the result on the left hand side of the separator.
*   Subtract the left hand side from the multiplier.

Example 1: Multiply 6543 by 9999.

Solution: Here, the number of digits in the multiplicand is equal to the number of 9s in the multiplier. As the rule suggests, the answer will have two parts.

Left side: Multiplicand – 1 = 6543 – 1 = 6542

Right side: 9 – 6 = 3, 9 – 5 = 4, 9 – 4 = 5 and, 9 – 2 = 7. Thus the right hand side will have 3457.

In order to simplify the calculation on the right hand side, we may subtract the result obtained in the left hand side from the multiplier.

Right hand side = 9999 – 6542 = 3457

Hence, 6543 × 9999 = 65423457

Example 2: Multiply 89654876 by 99999999.

Solution:

    Left side: 89654876 − 1 = 89654875
    Right side: 99999999 − 89654875 = 10345124
    Hence, 89654876 × 99999999 = 8965487510345124

Case 2: When the number of 9s in the multiplier is more than the number of digits in the multiplicand

Rule: In case 2, the same procedure will be applied as in case 1.

    Let us take a few examples.

Example 1: Multiply 56892 by 9999999.

Solution:

    Left side: 56892 − 1 = 56891
    Right side: 9999999 − 56891 = 9943108
    Hence, 56892 × 9999999 = 568919943108

Example 2: Multiply 324 by 99999999.

Solution:

    Left hand side = 324 − 1 = 323
    Right hand side = 99999999 − 323 = 99999676
    Hence, 324 × 99999999 = 32399999676

Case 3: When there are a lesser number of 9s in the multiplier than the number of digits in the multiplicand

In this case there is a little change in the method.

    First count the number of 9s in the multiplier. Mark as many numbers from right to left in the multiplicand. Subtract the remaining from the multiplicand to place it on the left hand side.

Take the complement of marked numbers from 100, 1000... and place them on the right hand side.

Finally, subtract 1 from the left hand side and this will be your new left hand side. Place it before the right hand side to get the answer.

Example 1: Multiply 147 by 99.

Solution: Since there are two 9s in the multiplier, 47 of the multiplicand should be marked or circled. The remaining 1 will first be subtracted and placed on the left hand side.

Left side: 147 − 1 = 146

Right side: Complement of marked or circled number 47

Now subtract the remaining digits i.e. 1 from the left side and write the complement of 47 on the right side.

Left side: 146 − 1 = 145

Right side: 100 − 47 = 53

Hence, 147 × 99 = 14553

Example 2: Multiply 259648 by 9999.

Solution: Since there are four 9s in the multiplier, four digits from right to left of multiplicand i.e. 9648 will be placed on the right side. On the left side, subtract 1 from the original number.

Left side: 259648 − 1 = 259647

Right side: Complement of 9648

Now subtract the remaining digits i.e. 25 from the left side, and write the complement of 47 on the right side.

Left side: 259647 − 25 = 259622

Right side: 10000 − 9648 = 0352

Hence, 259648 × 9999 = 2596220352

Urdhva Tiryagbhyam

This method is a panacea. It is applicable in all cases and there is no base required. You can multiply a 4-digit number by two digits. On first sight, you may not prefer this method, and find it tougher than the classroom method—but constant practice will make this easier every day. You will love this method as it reduces time and is applicable in finding squares by multiplying two polynomials. I shall not be dealing with a bigger number here as I have already discussed this method in detail in my previous book on Vedic Mathematics, *The Essentials of Vedic Mathematics*.

Let's begin.

Dot and Stick Method

Multiplication of 2-digit numbers

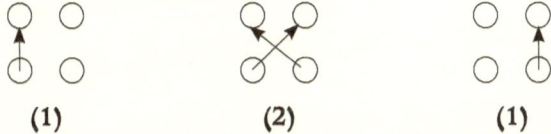

Multiplication of 3-digit numbers

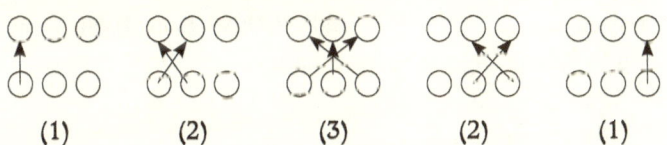

Multiplication of 4-digit numbers

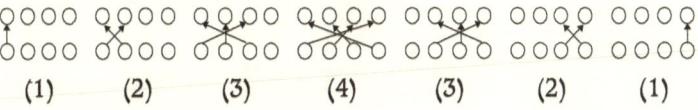

$$11 \times 11 = 121$$
$$111 \times 111 = 12321$$
$$1111 \times 1111 = 1234321$$
$$11111 \times 11111 = 123454321$$

The dot and stick method or Urdhva Tiryag method is the arrangement of dots on the multiple of recurrence of 1.

To multiply 2-digit numbers, square of 11 will be used and the dot arrangement will be 1 – 2 – 1.

To multiply 3-digit numbers, square of 111 will be used and the dot arrangement will be 1 – 2 – 3 – 2 – 1.

A. Multiplication of 2-digit numbers

Example 1: Multiply 76 by 42.

Solution:

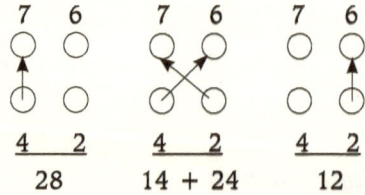

Arranging the numbers and adding them from right to left, taking only one digit at a time, we get the final result.

= 28 | 38 | 12

= 3192

Example 2: 58 × 34 = ?

Solution: Arranging the numbers on the dots.

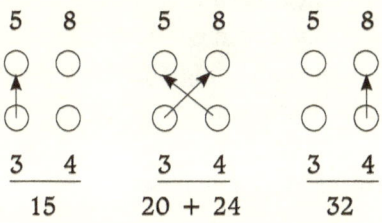

15	20 + 24	32

Arranging the numbers and adding them from right to left, taking only one digit at a time, we get the final result.

15 | 44 | 32

= 1972

Once the concept is clear, the whole process can be done mentally in one line.

Example 3: Multiply 77 by 39.

Solution: I do hope the dot and cross technique is clear to you. Here is the one line method. The sum of the cross multiplication of dots in the second stage has to be done mentally.

$$77$$
$$\times 39$$
$$= 21 \mid 84 \mid 63$$

= 3003

In the first vertical separator, $7 \times 9 = 63$ is written, in the second vertical separator the sum of the cross products of 7×9 and 3×7 is written directly:

i.e. $7 \times 9 + 3 \times 7 = 63 + 21 = 84$.

In the third vertical separator, $7 \times 3 = 21$ is placed. As told earlier, take only one digit from each section within a separator and add the remaining digit to the next group within the next separator as shown, in the direction of the arrow.

B. Multiplication of 3-digit numbers

Example 1: Multiply 566 by 281.

Solution:
Arrange the numbers on the dots as shown below.

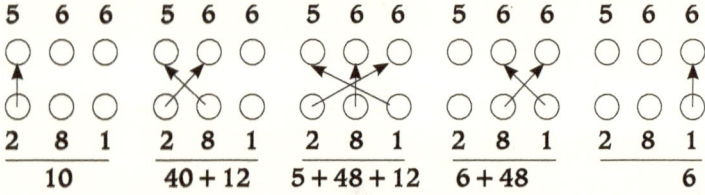

Arrange each set of numbers with a separator as shown below.

$$10 \mid 52 \mid 65 \mid 54 \mid 6$$

$= 159046$

Once you understand the process, you can do mental calculations and reduce the steps to a single line, without having to write down the number of dots.

Example 2: Multiply 247 by 989.

Solution: The whole operation of the dot and cross method is done here in one line.

```
            2 4 7
          × 9 8 9
    ₁8 | ₅2 | ₁₁3 | ₉2 | ₆3
      8    2    3    2    3
  + 1    5   11    9    6
  ─────────────────────────
    2    4    4    2    8    3
```

Before I wind up the chapter, let's take another example. Suppose you want to multiply a 3-digit number by a 2-digit number.

Example 3: Multiply 526 by 43.

Solution: This is a 3 × 2 digit multiplication so write a zero in front of 43, making it 043, and now apply the above 3 × 3 operation technique. Arrange the numbers on the dots as shown below.

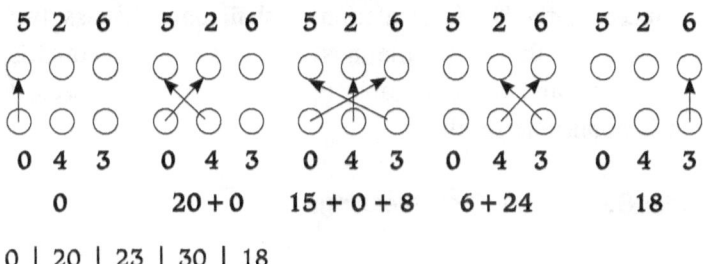

```
0 | 20 | 23 | 30 | 18
```

= 22618

I am wrapping up this chapter with the hope that you will explore other options yourself, and in case you want more examples with other options, you can read my previous book on Vedic Mathematics.

2

Square

Introduction

There are several methods to find the square of a number in Vedic Mathematics. The basic details of all the fundamental operations involved are already discussed in my book, *The Essentials of Vedic Mathematics*. Since this book contains the advanced methods of calculation, I shall only discuss two methods here that I love the most. The first Vedic method is conditional, and not applicable in all cases, but the second one is applicable to all.

Vedic Sutras and Their Meanings

1. **Yavadunam Tavaduni Kritya Vargena Yojayet** : This Vedic sub-sutra is used for squaring numbers which are closer to the base (10^n). This Vedic sutra simply says,
   a) Find the extent or deficiency of a number to be squared with respect to its base. This extent or deficiency is termed here as the **deviation**.
   b) Set up the square of the deviation at the end.
2. **Dwanda Yoga or Duplex Method:** The Duplex combination is applicable in all cases. The duplex of different

combinations of digits that will make calculation easy is discussed in this chapter.

Yavadunam Tavaduni Kritya Vargena Yojayet

This sutra works better when the number to be squared is near the base 10, 100, 1000...or is a multiple of the base i.e. 20, 30, 40...200, 300, 400...etc. Let us discover the squaring concept through this Vedic sub-sutra in two parts.

Case 1: When the number is near the base 10, 100, 1000...10^n

The answer is arrived at in two parts.

Left hand side of the separator = Number + Deviation

(Deviation may be positive or negative, depending on the base.)

Right hand side of the separator = Square of deviation

The right hand part of the separator will contain the same number of digits as the number of zeros in the base. The excess digits, if any, will be carried over to the left hand part, and the deficit digits, if any, will be filled up by putting the zeros to the left of the right hand part.

Example 1: Find the square of 12.

Solution: 12 is closer to base 10. Deviation = $12 - 10 = 2$.

$$(12)^2 = 12 + 2 \mid 2^2$$
$$= 14 \mid 4$$
$$= 144$$

Example 2: Find the square of 18.

Solution: 18 is closer to base 10. Deviation = 18 – 10 = 8.

$$(18)^2 = 18 + 8 \mid 8^2$$
$$= 26 \mid 64$$
$$= 26 + 6 \mid 4$$
$$= 324$$

Since Base = 10, the right hand part of the answer will contain a single digit.

Example 3: Find the square of 91.

Solution: 91 is closer to base 100. Deviation = 91 – 100 = – 9.

$$(91)^2 = 91 - 9 \mid (-9)^2$$
$$= 82 \mid 81$$
$$= 8281$$

Example 4: Find the square of 99.

Solution: 99 is closer to base 100. Deviation = 99 – 100 = – 1

$$(99)^2 = 99 - 1 \mid (-1)^2$$
$$= 98 \mid 1$$

Since Base = 100, the right hand part should have two digits, so one additional zero will be placed before 1.

Therefore, $(99)^2 = 9801$

Case 2: When the base is not in the form of 10^n, but a multiple of 10.

If the number to be squared is near the base 20, 30, 40...or 200, 300, 400...or 2000, 3000, 4000...the Yavadunam Tavduni sub-sutra will work with a slight change.

The answer will be arrived at in two parts.

The right hand part of the answer will be the square of the deviation from the base. The left hand part of the answer should be written with utmost care. Left hand part = (Number to be squared + Deviation) × sub-base.

Example 1: Find the square of 32.

Solution: 32 is closer to base 30.

Deviation = 32 − 30 = 2

$30 = 3 \times 10$

Sub-base = 3

Actual base = 10

$(32)^2 = (32 + 2) \times 3 \mid (2)^2$

$\qquad = 102 \mid 4$

$\qquad = 1024$

Example 2: Find the square of 47.

Solution: 47 is closer to base 50. Deviation = 47 − 50 = − 3

$50 = 5 \times 10$

Sub-base = 5

Actual base = 10

$(47)^2 = (47 - 3) \times 5 \mid (- 3)^2$

$\qquad = 220 \mid 9$

$\qquad = 2209$

As discussed in multiplication, here, too, you can use the same principle.

Base = 50 = 100 / 2

$(47)^2 = (47 - 3) / 2 \mid (- 3)^2$

$\qquad = 22 \mid 9$

$\qquad = 2209$

(Since 100 has two zeros, the right hand part should have two digits.)

Example 3: Find the square of 482.

Solution: 482 is closer to base 500.
Deviation = 482 − 500 = − 18

   500 = 5 × 100

   Sub-base = 5

   Actual base = 100

   $(482)^2 = (482 − 18) × 5 \mid (− 18)^2$

   $= 5 × 464 \mid 324$

   $= 2320 \mid 324$

   $= 232324$

Let us take the base 500 and find the square of 482 in another way.

   500 = 1000/2

   Hence, Base = 1000 and sub-base = ½

   Deviation = 482 − 500 = − 18

   $(482)^2 = (482 − 18) × ½ \mid (− 18)^2$

   $= 232 \mid 324$

   $= 232324$

Example 4: Find the square of 8989.

Solution: 8989 is closer to base 9000.

   Deviation = 8989 − 9000 = − 11

   9000 = 9 × 1000

   Sub-base = 9

   Actual base = 1000

   $(8989)^2 = (8989 − 11) × 9 \mid (− 11)^2$

   $= 9 × 8978 \mid 121$

   $= 80802 \mid 121$

   $= 80802121$

Duplex Method or Dwanda Yoga

The Dwanda Yoga or Duplex Method of squaring is one of the best squaring methods in Vedic Mathematics. After a little practice, you can find the square of any number mentally. This is unique in the sense that it has universal application. Let us denote the duplex of a number by D.

- Duplex of 1-digit number = Square of that number
  $D(a) = a^2$
  Duplex of $2 = 2^2 = 4$
  Duplex of $6 = 6^2 = 36$
- Duplex of 2-digit number = 2 × (product of digits)
  $D(ab) = 2ab$
  Duplex of $24 = 2 \times (2 \times 4) = 16$
  Duplex of $76 = 2 \times (7 \times 6) = 84$
- Duplex of 3-digit number = 2 × (1st digit × 3rd digit) + (square of middle digit)
  $D(abc) = 2ac + b^2$
  Duplex of $126 = 2 \times (1 \times 6) + 2^2 = 16$
  Duplex of $478 = 2 \times (4 \times 8) + 7^2 = 113$
- Duplex of 4-digit number = 2 × (1st digit × 4th digit) + 2 × (2nd digit × 3rd digit)
  $D(abcd) = 2ad + 2bc$
  Duplex of $2468 = 2 \times (2 \times 8) + 2 \times (4 \times 6) = 80$
  Duplex of $4567 = 2 \times (4 \times 7) + 2 \times (5 \times 6) = 116$

Once you learn to find the duplex of a number, you need to write the number in groups. The following pattern will help you in grouping the numbers.

$(11)^2 = 121$
$(1\ 1\ 1)^2 = 12321$
$(1\ 1\ 1\ 1)^2 = 1234321$
$(1\ 1\ 1\ 1\ 1)^2 = 23454321$
$(1\ 1\ 1\ 1\ 1\ 1)^2 = 12345654321$
$(1\ 1\ 1\ 1\ 1\ 1\ 1)^2 = 1234567654321$

Grouping of a number

The grouping of $(24)^2$ will follow the pattern of $(11)^2$.
    The groups for 24 are:

D(2)	D(24)	D(4)
1-digit	2-digit	1-digit

The grouping of $(245)^2$ will follow the pattern of $(111)^2$
    The groups of numbers for 245 are:

D(2)	D(24)	D(245)	D(45)	D(5)
1-digit	2-digit	3-digit	2-digit	1-digit

The grouping of $(2456)^2$ will follow the pattern of $(1111)^2$
    The groups of numbers for 2456 are:

D(2)	D(24)	D(245)	D(2456)	D(456)	D(56)	D(6)
1-digit	2-digit	3-digit	4-digit	3-digit	2-digit	1-digit

	Summary of the Duplex Method
1	$D(a) = a^2$
2	$D(ab) = 2ab$

3	$D(abc) = 2ac + b^2$
4	$D(abcd) = 2ad + 2bc$
5	$D(abcde) = 2ae + 2bd + c^2$
6	$D(abcdef) = 2af + 2be + 2cd$
7	$D(abcdefg) = 2ag + 2bf + 2ce + d^2$

How does the Duplex Method work?

- Form the groups of numbers to be squared as shown above.
- Write the duplex value for each group.
- Once the duplex value for each group is written, add the figures from right to left, keeping only one digit in each separator.

Example 1: Find the square of 32.

Solution: The groups for 32 are:

$$D(3) \qquad\qquad D(32) \qquad\qquad D(2)$$

$$= 3^2 \qquad\qquad |\ 2 \times 3 \times 2 \qquad\qquad |\ 2^2$$

$$= 9 \ |\ 1\ 2\ |\ 4$$

$$= 1024$$

Example 2: Find the square of 465.

Solution: The groups of numbers for 465 are:

$$D(4) \qquad D(46) \qquad D(465) \qquad D(65) \qquad D(5)$$

$$= 4^2 \quad 2 \times 4 \times 6 \quad 2 \times 4 \times 5 + 6^2 \quad 2 \times 6 \times 5 \quad 5^2$$

$$= 16 \mid 4 \; 8 \mid 7 \; 6 \mid 6 \; 0 \mid 2 \; 5$$

$$= 20 \mid {}_15 \mid {}_1 2 \mid 2 \mid 5$$
$$= 216225$$

Example 3: Find the square of 4856.

Solution: The groups for 4856 are:

4, 48, 485, 4856, 856, 56 and 6.

Duplex of 4 = 4^2 = 16

Duplex of 48 = 2 × 4 × 8 = 64

Duplex of 485 = 2 × 5 × 4 + 8^2 = 104

Duplex of 4856 = 2 × 4 × 6 + 2 × 8 × 5 = 128

Duplex of 856 = 2 × 8 × 6 + 5^2 = 121

Duplex of 56 = 2 × 5 × 6 = 60

Duplex of 6 = 6^2 = 36

Arrange the duplex of each number using separators.

$$= 16 \mid 64 \mid 104 \mid 128 \mid 121 \mid 60 \mid 36$$
$$= 23580736$$

You can extend the Duplex Method up to any number. Even squaring upto nine digits can be done using this method in a very short time. Explore it and enjoy.

3
Cube

Introduction

When a number is multiplied three times by itself, the number so obtained is called the cube of that number. For example, $a \times a \times a = a^3$. Here is the cube of the first ten numbers.

Number	1	2	3	4	5	6	7	8	9	10
Cube	1	8	27	64	125	216	343	512	729	1000

There are four methods to do cubing in Vedic Mathematics. As mentioned earlier, Vedic Mathematics enables you to experiment and choose the best method in a given situation. Besides Vedic Mathematics, there are some other techniques of easy cubing that you can learn in my book, *Speed Mathematics*.

The classroom method, as you know it, asks you to either multiply a given number three time or use the binomial expansion of the $(a + b)^3$ or $(a - b)^3$. Here, I will be exploring only two new methods of cubing through Vedic Mathematics.

Traditional method of cubing:

$(988)^3$ = 988 × 988 × 988

```
          9 8 8
        × 9 8 8
        7 9 0 4
      7 9 0 4 x
    8 8 9 2 x x
    9 7 6 1 4 4
        × 9 8 8
  7 8 0 9 1 5 2
7 8 0 9 1 5 2 x
8 7 8 5 2 9 6 x x
9 6 4 4 3 0 2 7 2
```

There is another traditional method that can be termed as better than the above method. The binomial expansion of $(a + b)^3$ and $(a - b)^3$ will reduce calculation time a bit, but this method is still not suitable as far as its application in competitive examinations is concerned.

a) $(988)^3 = (1000 - 12)^3 = (1000)^3 - 3(1000)^2 \times 12 + 3 \times 1000 \times (12)^2 - (12)^3$

$= 1000000000 - 36000000 + 432000 - 1728$

$= 964430272$

[Applying binomial expansion, $(a + b)^3 = a^3 - 3a^2b + 3ab^2 - b^3$]

b) $(108)^3 = (100 + 8)^3 = (100)^3 + 3 \times (100)^2 \times 8 + 3 \times 100 \times (8)^2 + (8)^3$

$= 1000000 + 240000 + 19200 + 512$

$= 1259712$

[Applying binomial expansion, $(a + b)^3 = a^3 + 3a^2b + 3ab^2 + b^3$]

Vedic sutra for cubing a number:

1. Anurupyen

Anurupyen Vedic Sutra is based on the concept of geometric progression. This method is best suited for cubing a small number comfortably. Though you can find the cube of a bigger number using this method, it involves a lot of calculations. In a geometric series, each successive number is the multiple of some constant ratio called **r**, or the common ratio.

If a = first term, r = common ratio, then the nth term $(t_n) = ar^{n-1}$

If a, b and c are in a geometric series, then,

R = second term/first term = third term/second term

$b/a = c/b$

or, $b^2 = ac$

Here are a few examples of geometric series.

    i) 2, 8, 32...

    ii) 5, 25, 125, 625...

In the first example, (i), a = first term and r = common ratio = 8/2 = 4

$t_n = 2\,(4)^{n-1} = 2 \times 2^{2(n-1)}$

In the second example, a = 5 and r = 5, hence $t_n = 5 \times (5)^{n-1}$

Rule:

- First, take the cube of the first digit (a) and multiply it with the common ratio (b/a), in a row of four figures.
- Double the second and third numbers and put them down below the second and third numbers. Finally, add up the two rows.

The Anurupyen method is just an extension of the above expansion. This can be simplified again if we take the help of geometric progression.

$$(ab)^3 = \begin{array}{cccc} a & ar & ar^2 & ar^3 \\ + & 2ar & 2ar^2 & \\ \hline a & 3ar & 3ar^2 & ar^3 \end{array} \quad \text{(where } r = b/a)$$

Let us take a few examples to understand the basic modus operandi.

Example 1: Find the cube of 12.

Solution: $(12)^3 = ?$
   Here, say $a = 1$ and $b = 2$
   r = common ratio = b/a = $2/1$ = 2

Hence the table arrangement will be as follows:

$$(12)^3 = \begin{array}{cccc} 1 & 2 & 4 & 8 \\ + & 4 & 8 & \\ \hline 1 & 7 & 2 & 8 \end{array}$$

Important points:

1. *If you start with the cube of the first digit and multiply with the geometric ratio up to the next three numbers, the fourth number of the series will be the cube of the second digit.*
2. *Addition should be done from right to left, keeping only a single digit at a time and the remaining digit will be carried over to the next column, and so on.*

Example 2: Find the cube of 19.

Solution: $(19)^3 = ?$
    Here, say $a = 1$ and $b = 9$
    r = common ratio = $b/a = 9/1 = 9$

Hence the table arrangement will be as follows:

1	9	81	729
	18	162	
1	2 7	24 3	72 9

$$= 6 8 5 9$$

Example 3: Find the cube of 29.

Solution:
    Here, say $a = 2$ and $b = 9$
    r = common ratio = $b/a = 9/2$

Hence the table arrangement will be as follows:

8	36	162	729
	72	324	
8	10 8	48 6	729

$$= 24389$$

[First column = Cube of first number = a^3
    Second column = ar
    Third column = ar^2
    Fourth column = $ar^3 = b$

Example 4: Find the cube of 32.

Solution: $(32)^3 = ?$

Here, say a = 3 and b = 2

r = common ratio = b/a = 2/3

Hence the first line of the table arrangement will be as follows:

$$(32)^3 = 3^3 \ (27) \ 27 \times 2/3 \ (18) \ 18 \times 2/3 \ (12) \ 12 \times 2/3 \ (8)$$

	27	18	12	8
=		36	24	
=	2 7	5 4	3 6	8

= 3 2 7 6 8

Example 5: Find the cube of 46.

Solution: $(46)^3 = ?$

Here say a = 4 and b = 6

r = common ratio = b/a = 6/4

Hence, the table arrangement will be as follows:

$$(46)^3 = 4^3 \ (= 64) \ 64 \times 6/4 \ (= 96) \ 96 \times 6/4 \ (= 144)$$
$$144 \times 8/9 \ (= 512)$$

	64	96	144	216
		192	288	
	64	288	432	216
=	64	288	432	216
=	64	288	453	6
=	64	333	3	6

= 97336

Example 6: Find the cube of 96.

Solution:

$$(96)^3 = \begin{array}{cccc} 729 & 486 & 324 & 216 \\ & 972 & 648 & \\ \hline 729 & 1458 & 972 & 216 \end{array}$$

$$= 729 + 145/8 + 97/2 + 21/6$$

$$= 884736$$

Example 7: Find the cube of 105.

Solution: $(105)^3 = ?$

Here a = 10 and b = 5, hence common ratio = 5/10 = 1/2

$$(105)^3 = \begin{array}{cccc} 1000 & 500 & 250 & 125 \\ + & 1000 & 500 & \\ \hline 1000 & 1500 & 750 & 125 \end{array}$$

Simple addition, as done in the above example, will give you the wrong answer. Now, the big question is, what next?

The answer is very simple.

1000000 + 150000 + 7500 + 125 = 1157625

If the number is between 100 and 999, put 1, 2 and 3 zeros in the 2nd, 3rd and 4th column of the result obtained.

In case the number is above 1000, you need to put 2, 4 and 6 zeros after each digit.

In the second column from right we have 750, so it will become 7500 after adding 1 zero.

In the third column from right we have 1500, so after putting 2 zeros, it will become 150000.

In the fourth column from right, we have 1000, so add three zeros and it becomes 1000000.

Let us find the cube of a number above 1000.

Example 8: Find the cube of 1001.

Solution:
Here, a = 10 and b = 01, hence common ratio = 01/10 = 1/10

$$(1001)^3 = \quad \begin{array}{cccc} 1000 & 100 & 10 & 1 \\ + & 200 & 20 & \\ \hline 1000 & 300 & 30 & 1 \end{array}$$

Since the number is above 1000, start putting 6, 4 and 2 zeros from the extreme left before adding. Once the process of putting zeros is complete, you can simply add to get the result.

$(1001)^3 = 1000000000 + 3000000 + 3000 + 1 = 1003003001$

2. Nikhilam Vedic Sutra

Rule: This method works better if the number to be cubed is near the base, which is either a multiple or a power of 10.

- First, take the deviation of the number to be cubed from its base. The base should be the multiple of 10. If the base is 10, 100, 1000...then sub-base = 1; on the other hand, if the base = 40, then sub-base = 4, because 40 = 4 × 10
- The whole cubing process then involves three steps.
  A) (Number to be cubed + 2 × deviation from the base) × (sub-base)^2
  B) {3 × (deviation)^2} × sub-base
  C) (Deviation)^3
- If there is no sub-base, then the calculation becomes very easy.

Let us look at some examples.

Example 1: Find the cube of 25 using Nikhilam Sutra.

Solution: 25 is nearer to the base 20 (2 × 10), hence

Deviation = 25 − 10 = 5, sub-base = 2

$$(25)^3 = \underbrace{[25 + 2 \times 5 \times 2^2] \times 2}_{\text{1st term}} \mid \underbrace{3 \times (5)^2}_{\text{2nd term}} \mid \underbrace{(5)^3}_{\text{3rd term}}$$

$\quad = 140 \mid 150 \mid 125$

$\quad = 140 \mid 150 + 12 \mid 5$

$\quad = 140 \mid 162 \mid 5$

$\quad = 140 + 16 \mid 2 \mid 5$

$\quad = 156 \mid 2 \mid 5$

$\quad = 15625$

Example 2: Find the cube of 58 by using Nikhilam Sutra.

Solution: 58 = 5 × 10 + 8

base = 10   sub-base = 10   and excess = 8

Hence $(58)^3 = \underbrace{[58 + 2 \times (8)] \times 5^2}_{\text{1st term}} \mid \underbrace{3 \times (8)^2 \times 5}_{\text{2nd term}} \mid \underbrace{(8)^3}_{\text{3rd term}}$

$\quad = 1850 \mid 960 \mid 512$

$\quad = 1850 \mid 1011 \mid 2$

$\quad = 1951 \mid 1 \mid 2$

Hence $(58)^3 = 195112$

Example 3: Find the cube of 98 by using Nikhilam Sutra.

Solution: 98 is nearer to the base 100.

Deviation = 98 − 100 = − 2

Hence $(98)^3 = \underbrace{98 + 2 \times (-2)}_{\text{1st term}} \mid \underbrace{3 \times (-2)^2}_{\text{2nd term}} \mid \underbrace{(-2)^3}_{\text{3rd term}}$

$\quad = 94 \mid 12 \mid - 8$

$$= 94 \mid 11 \mid 100 - 8$$
$$= 94 \mid 11 \mid 92$$

Hence $(98)^3 = 941192$

Example 4: Find the cube of 104 by using Nikhilam Sutra.

Solution: Working base = 100

Deviation = $104 - 100 = 4$

$$(104)^3 = 104 + 4 \times 2 \mid 3 \times 4^2 \mid 4^3$$
$$= 112 \mid 48 \mid 64$$
$$= 1124864$$

(Since the base = 100, there should be two digits in between each digit separator.)

Let's solve some questions in a single line approach and enjoy the beauty of Vedic Mathematics.

Example 1: Find the cube of 990.

Solution: Deviation = $990 - 1000 = -10$

$$(990)^3 = 990 - 20 \mid 3 \times 100 \mid -1000$$
$$= 970 \mid 300 \mid -1000$$
$$= 970 \mid 299 \mid 000$$

Example 2: Find the cube of 1997.

Solution: Deviation = $1997 - 2000 = -3$

$$(1997)^3 = (1997\ldots - 2 \times 3) \times 2^2 \mid 3 \times (-3)^2 \mid (-3)^3$$
$$= 7964 \mid 054 \mid -027$$
$$= 7964 \mid 054 - 1 \mid 1000 - 027$$
$$= 7964 \mid 053 \mid 973$$
$$= 7694053973$$

[Since the last column has a negative sign, so 1 is subtracted from the previous column and the negative column is subtracted from the base. 054 in second column becomes $054 - 1 = 053$.

– 027 in third column becomes 1000 – 027 = 973]

The three Vedic sutras discussed here give you room to choose the best for a particular problem. If the number to be cubed is near a given base which is a power of 10 or a multiple of 10 then you have different options to decide what to use. Moreover, there are other Vedic methods you can use in a particular situation, but for those, you have to read a basic book on Vedic Mathematics. In a competitive examination, you need to learn the cube of numbers up to 30 and you can see how effective Vedic Mathematics is in extracting the cube of even a larger number. So, explore more with lots of examples and gain mastery over the subject.

PART II

4

Highest Common Factor of Polynomials

Introduction

The HCF (Highest Common Factor) or GCD (Greatest Common Divisor) of two or more numbers is obtained by the prime factorization method or by the division method. In the prime factorization method, we express the given number in terms of its prime factors and write down the smallest power of each of the prime factors common to all the given numbers. The continued products of these that is common to all the numbers, gives the HCF.

Example 1: Find the HCF of 12 and 24.

Solution: $12 = 2 \times 2 \times 3$

$24 = 2 \times 2 \times 2 \times 3$

As we can see, the common prime factors are 2, 2 and 3.

$HCF = 2 \times 2 \times 3 = 12$

The division method is easy and works effectively.

a) Divide the larger number by the smaller one and get a remainder.

b) Divide the previous divisor by the remainder obtained.

c) Repeat the process until you get the remainder as zero.

d) The last divisor is the HCF.

Example 2: Find the HCF of 108 and 162.

Answer:

$$108) \overline{162} (1$$
$$- \underline{108}$$
$$54) \overline{108} (2$$
$$- \underline{108}$$
$$0$$

HCF = 54

Similarly, the HCF of polynomials can be obtained using

a) Long division method,
b) Factorization.

Here we shall first focus on how the HCF of two polynomials can be obtained using the Vedic method.

Example 3: Find the HCF of 15 and 20.

Solution: $15 = 3 \times 5$
$$20 = 2 \times 2 \times 5$$
Therefore, HCF (15, 20) = 5

Generally, to determine HCF, we find the common factor in all the numbers whose HCF is to be found. The same thing is true even for polynomials. First, we break down each polynomial into its factors and then try to find the common factor of each.

Example 1: Find the HCF of $x^2 + 6x + 8$ and $x^2 + x - 12$.

Solution: Let us first find the factors of these two polynomials.

$$P(x) = x^2 + 6x + 8$$
$$= (x + 2) (x + 4)$$
$$Q(x) = x^2 + x - 12$$
$$= (x + 4) (x - 3)$$

Therefore, HCF = $x + 4$

Example 2: Find the HCF of $x^3 + 1$ and $x^2 - 1$.

Solution: Let us factorize the two polynomials.

$$P(x) = x^3 + 1 = (x + 1) (x^2 - x + 1)$$
$$Q(x) = x^2 - 1$$
$$= (x + 1) (x - 1)$$

Hence, HCF = $x - 1$

The above two examples explore the method of finding the HCF of two polynomials the way it is taught in our modern classrooms. Let's explore the Vedic approach of finding the HCF.

The Vedic approach uses 3 sutras:

a) Lopana–Sthapana
b) Sakalana–Vyavkalana
c) Adyamadhya

How it works

*   The Vedic approach first breaks the power of the given polynomials. In order to do this, we first regroup the polynomials and try to destroy the highest power. This can be done by adding or subtracting the two polynomials after balancing the highest power in each polynomial.
*   We then remove the common factor, if any, from each polynomial, and this is the HCF of the given polynomials.

Example 1: Find the HCF of $x^2 + 6x + 8$ and $x^2 + x - 12$.

Solution: Apply the Sakalana–Vyavkalana method and remove the power of the polynomials.

$x^2 + 6x + 8$ and $x^2 + x - 12$	Adding and	$x^2 + 6x + 8$
$x^2 + 6x + 8$	subtracting the	$x^2 + x - 12$
$x^2 + x - 12$	polynomials, we get:	$2x^2 + 7x - 4$
$5x + 20 = (x + 4)$		$= 2x^2 + 8x - x - 4$
		$= 2x (x + 4) - 1 (x + 4)$
		$= (2x - 1) (x + 4)$

Therefore, the HCF = $x + 4$.

The interesting part of this method is that you need not do both addition and subtraction in order to reach the exact answer. Even the single operation will yield results.

Let's look at a few examples.

Example 2: Find the HCF of $x^2 + 5x + 4$ and $x^2 + 7x + 6$.

Solution: Since the coefficients of the highest power in both the polynomials are the same, we simply get the answer using the Lopana–Sthanpana method in this case.

$$\text{Subtract} \begin{cases} x^2 + 5x + 4 \\ x^2 + 7x + 6 \\ \hline -2) - 2x - 2 \end{cases}$$
$$x + 1$$

$(x^2 + 5x + 4) - (x^2 + 7x + 6) = -2x - 2 = -2 (x + 1)$

Example 3: Find the HCF of $x^3 - 3x^2 - 4x + 12$ and $x^3 - 7x^2 + 16x - 12$.

Solution:

$x^3 - 3x^2 - 4x + 12$
$x^3 - 7x^2 + 16x - 12$

$2x^3 - 10x^2 + 20x$

$= 2x(x^2 - 5x + 10)$

Therefore, the HCF $= (x^2 - 5x + 10)$

Example 4: Find the HCF of $x^3 - 7x - 6$ and $x^3 + 8x^2 + 17x + 10$.

Solution: Subtract the two polynomials to get the HCF.

$$\begin{array}{r} x^3 \qquad - 7x - 6 \\ x^3 + 8x^2 + 17x + 10 \\ \hline - 8x^2 - 24x - 16 \end{array}$$

$= -8(x^2 + 3x + 2)$

Hence, HCF is $x^2 + 3x + 2$.

Example 5: Find the HCF of $6x^4 - 7x^3 - 5x^2 + 14x + 7$ and $3x^3 - 5x^2 + 7$.

Solution: On the very first observation, we find that the first polynomial has the power of 4 and the second one the power of 3. The common method of finding the HCF in this case is difficult, as finding a factor of a biquadratic is hard. Let's do it the Vedic way.

First multiply the second expression by 2x so that the degree of the second polynomial is also the same as that of the first polynomial. Moreover, if the coefficients of both the polynomials are not the same, then multiply them by some number or variable or both, to make the coefficient of the highest degree the same in both the polynomials.

$$\begin{aligned} P(x) &= 6x^4 - 7x^3 - 5x^2 + 14x + 7 \\ Q(x) &= 3x^3 - 5x^2 + 7 \\ &= 2x\,(3x^3 - 5x^2 + 7) \qquad \text{[multiplying by 2x]} \\ &= 6x^4 - 10x^3 + 14x \end{aligned}$$

Now, subtracting these polynomials,

$$6x^4 - 7x^3 - 5x^2 + 14x + 7$$
$$\underline{6x^4 - 10x^3 \qquad + 14x}$$
$$3x^3 - 5x^2 \qquad\quad + 7$$
$$\text{HCF} = 3x^3 - 5x^2 + 7$$

As you have seen in the above examples, the HCF of two polynomials can be easily found by subtracting the two polynomials, as well as by adding them. You are the best judge to decide which operation you are comfortable with, in the given situation.

Let's look at an example.

Example 6: Find the HCF of $2x^3 + x^2 - 9$ and $x^4 + 2x^2 + 9$.

Solution: Like the previous example, here, too, we have two polynomials with different degrees. But minute observation will tell you how to proceed further. As the constant term in both the polynomials is the same, simple addition will make finding the HCF easier.

Let's first do it by addition.

$$P(x) = x^4 + 2x^2 + 9$$
$$\underline{Q(x) = 2x^3 + x^2 - 9}$$
$$= x^4 + 2x^3 + 3x^2$$
$$= x^2(x^2 + 2x + 3)$$

Hence, HCF $= x^2 + 2x + 3$

Since we can't factorize it further, we stop here. Let's solve the same question by the method of subtraction.

$$P(x) = x^4 + 2x^2 + 9$$
$$\underline{Q(x) = 2x^3 + x^2 - 9}$$

Multiply Q(x) by x and P(x) by 2 to make the coefficient of the highest power the same, and then subtract them.

$$P(x) = 2x^4 + 4x^2 + 18$$
$$\underline{Q(x) = 2x^4 + x^3 - 9x}$$
$$= -x^3 + 4x^2 + 9x + 18 \quad \text{...(1)}$$

As we can see, the difference of the two polynomials after balancing them can still be factorized, so we need one more operation to reach the final answer.

Since the difference has the highest power of 3, we add the polynomials having the power of 3.

We have $Q(x) = 2x^3 + x^2 - 9$.

Multiply the difference of the polynomials termed as expression (1) by 2 and add it with Q(x) so that both the polynomials have a similar first term such as degree and coefficients.

$$-2x^3 + 8x^2 + 18x + 36$$
$$\underline{2x^3 + x^2 \qquad\qquad -9}$$
$$= 9x^2 + 18x + 27$$
$$= 9(x^2 + 2x + 3)$$

Hence, HCF = $x^2 + 2x + 3$.

Example 7: Find the HCF of $2x^2 - x - 3$ and $2x^2 + x - 6$.

Solution: Since the first terms of both the polynomials are the same, we simply need to subtract one from the other.

$$2x^2 - x - 3$$
$$\underline{2x^2 + x - 6}$$
$$-2x + 3$$
$$= -1\,(2x - 3)$$

Example 8: Find the HCF of $6x^4 - 11x^3 + 16x^2 - 22x + 8$ and $6x^4 - 11x^3 - 8x^2 + 22x - 8$.

Solution: Since the powers of both the polynomials are the same, so are the coefficients of the highest order. Let's first subtract these two polynomials.

$$
\begin{array}{r}
6x^4 - 11x^3 + 16x^2 - 22x + 8 \\
\underline{6x^4 - 11x^3 - 8x^2 + 22x - 8} \\
24x^2 - 44x + 16
\end{array}
$$

$$= 4(6x^2 - 11x + 4)$$

Therefore, HCF $= 6x^2 - 11x + 4$.

Enjoy the Vedic technique of HCF of polynomials. Keep practising more and more to have a better understanding of the concept.

5

Multiplication of Polynomials

Introduction

In my first book on Vedic Mathematics, *The Essentials of Vedic Mathematics*, I focused on 8 Vedic sutras used in different scenarios to multiply two, three or four numbers. The most important among them all was the Urdhva Tiryagbhyam sutra, or what I have named as the Dot and Stick method. The same sutra will be beneficial here in multiplying two polynomials under different categories.

- Multiplication of binomials
- Multiplication of polynomials with an equal number of terms
- Multiplication of polynomials with an unequal number of terms

Let us look at an example of multiplication with the Dot and Stick method.

Example: $92 \times 18 = ?$

Solution: Arranging the numbers on the dots.

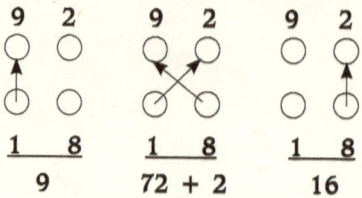

Arranging the numbers and adding them from right to left, taking only one digit at a time, we get the final result.

$$= 9 \mid 74 \mid 16$$

$$= 1656$$

Vedic Method of Multiplying Polynomials

If you want to learn more about the working of the Dot and Stick method, do read the multiplication chapter in detail, and if you are curious to learn different multiplication techniques, then remember to read my most popular book, *The Essentials of Vedic Mathematics*. A brief note on how to place numbers/coefficients on the dots is shown here. The basic difference between plain multiplication and multiplication in algebra is that in multiplication of polynomials, you don't need to shift the number into the previous column as shown above. Every individual operation is an independent operation and need not be moved or placed in other columns.

Multiplication of Binomial Equations

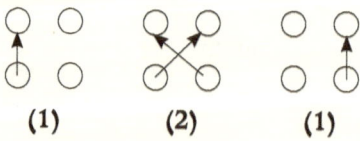

(1)   (2)   (1)

Multiplication of Trinomials

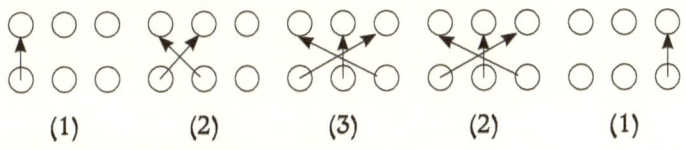

(1)   (2)   (3)   (2)   (1)

Case 1: Multiplication of Binomials

In a binomial expression, we have two terms—either both are variables, or there is one variable and one constant.

Example, $2x + 3y$ and $3y - 4$

Let's look at how Vedic Mathematics helps in multiplication.

Example: Multiply $x + 2y$ and $3x + 4y$.

Solution: Let us first understand it in the traditional way.

$$x + 2y$$
$$\times\ 3x + 4y$$
$$= 4y\ (x + 2y) + 3x\ (x + 2y)\ \text{(Distributive law)}$$
$$= 4xy + 8y^2 + 3x^2 + 6xy$$
$$= 3x^2 + 10xy + 8y^2$$

Vedic method

Before I proceed with the Vedic method, let me explain to you the steps involved in solving such an equation.

Step 1: First, write the two variables on the top and put the coefficients from each equation below. Apply the Urdhya Tiryagbhyam Vedic sutra.

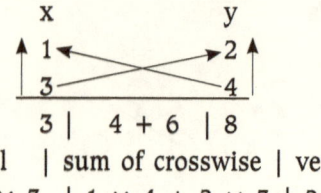

$$3 \mid \quad 4 + 6 \quad \mid 8$$

Vertical | sum of crosswise | vertical

$$1 \times 3 \mid 1 \times 4 + 2 \times 3 \mid 2 \times 4$$

$$3 \mid 10 \mid 8$$

Step 2: Starting from the right, add the variables to these coefficients in the following manner.

a) The vertical multiplication of y and y is 8. So add y^2 to 8, as this is the coefficient of y^2.

b) The crosswise multiplication of x and y yields the result 10, so add xy to 10.

c) The vertical multiplication of x and x yields 3, so this is the coefficient of x^2.

Therefore our answer is $3x^2 + 10xy + 8y^2$

Example 1: Multiply $(5x - 3y)$ by $(2x - 7y)$.

Solution:

Step 1: Write the two variables on top and their coefficients, along with their respective signs, below them.

Step 2: Do vertical and crosswise multiplication from the right. The multiplication will have the following steps:

a) $5 \times 2 = 10$ (vertical product)

b) $5 \times -7 + 2 \times (-3) = -35 - 6 = 41$ (sum of cross wise multiplication)

c) $-3 \times -7 = 21$ (vertical product)

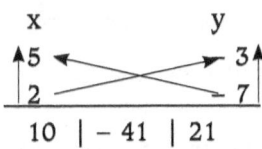

$$10 \mid -41 \mid 21$$

Step 3: Place the respective variables next to the coefficients, i.e.,

Place y^2 next to 21,

xy next to -41,

and x^2 next to 10.

Hence the result is:

$(5x - 3y) \times (2x - 7y) = 10x^2 - 41xy + 21y^2$

Example 2: Multiply $3x - 7y$ by $2x - 5y$.

Solution: Vedic multiplication involves the following steps.

Step 1: Write down the variable at the top and its respective coefficient below, with the proper sign.

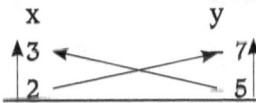

Step 2: Do vertical and crosswise multiplication from the right and place the proper variables next to the coefficients.

a) $-7 \times -5 = 35$ (vertical product and coefficient of y^2)

b) $3 \times -5 + 2 \times -7 = -29$ (crosswise product and coefficient of xy)

c) $3 \times 2 = 6$ (vertical product of extreme left and coefficient of x^2)

Hence the product is

$$(3x - 7y) \times (2x - 5y) = 6x^2 - 29xy + 35y^2$$

The above examples might look like they are time-consuming at first glance, but these have been elaborated for better understanding of the facts. The whole operation can be completed in a single line once you have enough practice. Let's see how we can work out the answer in a single line.

Rules:

- Write down the variable at the top
- Place the coefficients below the variables with the respective sign (+ or –).
- Multiply the number by the vertical and crosswise method as shown above and also discussed in the multiplication chapter. Remember one thing—don't take forward any carry over as done in usual multiplication.
- Place the respective variables next to the coefficients to get the one-line answer.

Example 3: Multiply $(2x + 3y)$ by $(11x + 5y)$.

Solution:

$$= 22x^2 + 43xy + 15y^2$$

Example 4: Multiply $2y^2 - 4z$ and $3y^2 - 7z$.

Solution:

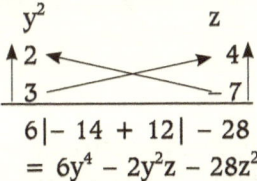

$$= 6y^4 - 2y^2z - 28z^2$$

Since $y^2 \times y^2 = y^4$, 6 is obviously the coefficient of y^4. Moreover, the crosswise multiplication gives the coefficient -2 and it is the coefficient of y^2z. The extreme right vertical multiplication (-28) is the coefficient of $z \times z = z^2$.

If you look at the method minutely you will find that we are exploring the formula:

$$(x + a)(x + b) = x^2 + (a + b)x + ab$$

First multiply the left coefficients, cross multiply and add the coefficients and finally multiply the coefficient on the right side.

Case 2: Multiplication of Trinomials

An algebraic expression involving three terms is called a trinomial, e.g. $x^2 + 2x + 3$.

Vedic method Urdhva Tiryagbhyam is applicable to the polynomial involving a different power of x as well.

Rules:

1. Write the variables above the horizontal line and then list the coefficients of the variables with the respective signs below them.

2. Perform the vertical and crosswise multiplication of the coefficients.

3. Add the variables to the coefficients in their respective order.

Example 1: Multiply $(x^2 + 2x + 3)$ by $(3x^2 + 2x + 4)$.

Solution: This polynomial of the second degree involves two variables, namely x^2, x and one independent term. Place x^0 for the independent term. Write the variables at the top and put down the coefficients below the variables shown here.

x^2	x	x^0
1	2	3
3	2	4

I am hopeful that the above arrow diagram as discussed in the multiplication chapter under Urdhva Tiryagbhyam sutra will help you in understanding the algebraic multiplication effortlessly. I am also listing the step-by-step procedure for easy understanding.

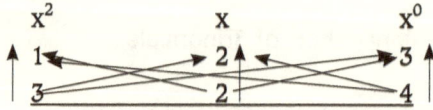

Step 1: Do the vertical and crosswise multiplication from the right as shown in the above diagram. The method has been explicitly explained below.

a) $3 \times 4 = 12$

b) $2 \times 4 + 2 \times 3 = 14$

c) $1 \times 4 + 3 \times 3 + 2 \times 2 = 17$

d) $1 \times 2 + 3 \times 2 = 8$

e) $1 \times 3 = 3$

Step 2: Place these coefficients below in the answer line column.

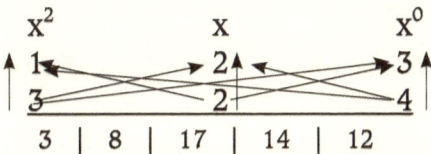

$$x^2 \qquad\qquad x \qquad\qquad x^0$$

1 → 2 ← 3
3 — 2 — 4

3 | 8 | 17 | 14 | 12

Starting from the extreme right, place the variable next to each coefficient in increasing order, i.e., place x^0 close to 12, x^1 close to 14, x^2 close to 17, x^3 close to 8 and x^4 close to 3.

Hence, $(x^2 + 2x + 3) \times (3x^2 + 2x + 4) = 3 x^4 + 8x^3 + 17x^2 + 14x + 12$

Example 2: Multiply $2x^2 - 4x + 6$ by $3x^2 - 7x - 2$.

Solution:

Step 1: Put the variable x^2, x and x^0 at the top and place the coefficient of the polynomials below it along with the respective sign.

x^2	x	x^0
2	-4	6
3	-7	-2

Step 2: Do the vertical and crosswise multiplication from the right. The steps are shown here for clarity and better understanding.

$$x^2 \qquad\qquad x \qquad\qquad x^0$$

2 ← 4 ← 6
3 — −7 — −2

a) $6 \times -2 = -12$
b) $-4 \times -2 + 6 \times -7 = -34$

c) $2 \times -2 + 3 \times 6 + (-4) \times (-7) = 42$

d) $2 \times -7 + 3 \times -4 = -26$

e) $2 \times 3 = 6$

Step 3: Place the coefficient obtained in Step 2 below in the answer line. Starting from the extreme right i.e., (-12), place the variable close to each successive coefficient in increasing order.

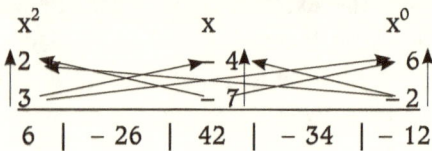

The variables placed next to the coefficients are shown here.

x^0 or no variable next to -12, x next to -34, x^2 next to 42, x^3 next to -26 and x^4 next to 6.

Hence $(2x^2 - 4x + 6) \times (3x^2 - 7x - 2) = 6x^4 - 26x^3 + 42x^2 - 34x - 12$.

Case 3: Polynomials having an unequal number of terms

When we talk about an unequal number of terms, it simply means that we are going to multiply two polynomials, one having greater and other having a lesser number of terms. The rule will remain the same, but you need to do a little modification while writing the polynomial one below another. Simply place a zero as the coefficients for the variables missing. Let us understand this with an example.

Example 1: Multiply $7x^2 + 6x + 5$ by $x + 9$.

Since the second equation involves only two terms i.e. x and 9, and the first equation has three terms, namely $7x^2$, 6x and 5, this gives us a clue that the x^2 term is missing in the second equation. Hence we shall write the second equation as:

$x + 9 = 0x^2 + x + 9$

Now the multiplication of the above equations will be done like the previous case.

Step 1: Put the variables x^2, x and x^0 at the top, and the coefficients of the variables with their respective signs below it.

x^2	x	x^0
7	6	5
0	1	9

Step 2: Do the vertical and crosswise multiplication.

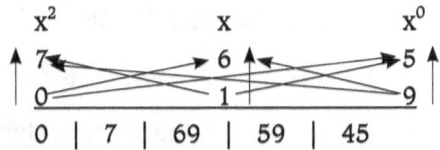

0 | 7 | 69 | 59 | 45

Step 3: Place the respective sign and start placing the variables from right to left, increasing the power of the variables in each preceding term,

i.e. x^0 next to 45, x^1 next to 59, x^2 next to 69 and x^3 next to 7.

Hence, $(7x^2 + 6x + 5) \times (x + 9) = 7x^3 + 69x^2 + 59x + 45$

Example 2: Multiply $2x^2 - 7$ by $3x^2 + 4x$.

Step 1: Place the variables and their corresponding coefficients with their respective signs as shown here.

x^2	x	x^0
2	0	-7

| 3 | 4 | 0 |

Step 2: Do the vertical and crosswise multiplication.

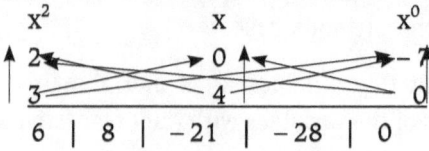

6 | 8 | – 21 | – 28 | 0

Step 3: Place the variables in ascending order from the right to left.

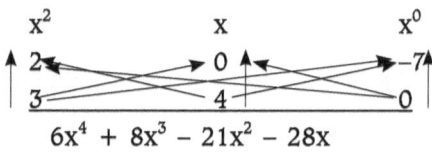

$6x^4 + 8x^3 - 21x^2 - 28x$

Hence, $(2x^2 - 7) \times (3x^2 + 4x) = 6x^4 + 8x^3 - 21x^2 - 28x$

After going through the Vedic method of multiplying binomials, trinomials etc. you must have noticed the similarity of operations in the Urdhvatiryag method of multiplication. Multiplication of polynomials will not be difficult if you practice at least five sums of each type, and once you are done, you can do the whole operation in a single line without writing the detailed operations. So, keep practising, as this is the mantra of success.

6

Division of Polynomials

Introduction

In order to find the factor of a polynomial, we apply the division principle. Let's suppose we have a polynomial, $x^3 + 1$, and we have one of its factors as $x + 1$, then the other factor can be obtained by simply dividing it. In algebra, we basically apply two important theorems to check whether the polynomial is factorable or not. Let me tell you what the two theorems are first.

- a) Factor Theorem
- b) Remainder Theorem

Factor Theorem:

If $p(x)$ is a polynomial and is divided by $x - a$, then if $p(a) = 0$ then $x - a$ will be its factor.

$$x - 2 \overline{\smash{\big)}\ x^3 + 4x^2 - 5x - 14}$$

$$\begin{array}{r} x^2 + 6x + 7 \\ x - 2 \overline{\smash{\big)}\ x^3 + 4x^2 - 5x - 14} \\ \underline{-x^3 + 2x^2} \\ 6x^2 + 5x \\ \underline{-6x^2 + 12x} \\ 7x + 14 \\ \underline{-7x + 14} \\ 0 \end{array}$$

Here, $x - 2$ is the factor of polynomial $p(x) = x^3 + 4x^2 - 5x - 14$

Remainder Theorem:

If $p(x)$ is a polynomial and is divided by $x - a$, then the remainder will be $f(a)$.

Example: If $3x^2 - 7x + 11$ is divided by $x - 2$, then find the remainder.

Solution: $p(x) = 3x^2 - 7x + 11$
$p(2) = 3(2)^2 - 7 \times 2 + 11 = 9$

As you have seen, dividing a polynomial is a long process, but with the help of the Vedic sutras, Paravartya Yojayet and Nikhilam method, we can divide polynomials in a very simple way. Let us look at one example of the Nikhilam method of division.

Example: Divide 10025 by 88.

Solution: Base = 100
   Complement = $100 - 88 = 12$

Column 1			Column 2 (Q)			Column 3 (R)	
Divisor	8	8	1	0	0	2	5
Complement =	1	2		1	2	–	–
						2	–
			↓	↓	↓	3	6
			1	1	3	8	1

Hence,

    Quotient = 113

    Remainder = 81

(To study simple and straight division further, you may refer to *The Essentials of Vedic Mathematics*.)

Let's look at an example of the Paravartya Yojayet method. In the Nikhilam method, the difference from the base is written as it is, whereas in Paravartya, the difference is written with each digit with a negative sign in the revised complement.

Example: Divide 239479 by 11213.

Solution: Base = 10000

    Complement = 11213 – 10000 = 1213

    Complement with changed sign for each digit = – 1 – 2 – 1 – 3

Since the base has four zeros, arrange the digits in the quotient and remainder columns accordingly.

	Column 1	Column 2 (Q)		Column 3 (R)				
Divisor	1 1 2 1 3	2	3	9	4	7	9	
Complement =	1 2 1 3		– 2	– 4	– 2	– 6	– 0	(Revised complement × 2)
Revised Complement =	– 1 – 2 – 1 – 3			– 1	– 2	– 1	– 3	(Revised complement × 1)
		2	1	4	0	0	6	

Quotient = 21

Remainder = 4006

In dividing polynomials, we shall use the Paravartya Yojayet method.

(To know more about Paravartya Yojayet, you may refer to my book, *The Essentials of Vedic Mathematics*.)

Working method:

- First put the divisor as equal to zero. Put it in the first column.
- The dividend should be written in descending order of power. In case any term is missing, put in a zero to fill in for the missing term. In the dividend column, put only the coefficient of polynomials and not the whole term.
- Carry down the first number of dividends.
- Multiply the number placed in the divisor column by the first leading coefficient carried down, and put the result in the next column.
- Add the two numbers together and write the result at the bottom.
- Repeat the same steps till you reach the end of the problem.
- The bottom row gives the answer. The last number of the bottom row is the remainder, and the remaining is the quotient of the polynomial. Starting from the left, put the power of the variable as one less than the original power, and go down by one with each term.

Example 1: Divide $2x^3 - 5x^2 + 3x + 7$ by $x - 2$

Solution:

a) As stated above, first put the denominator as equal to zero.

If x – 2 = 0

⇒x = 2 (this is the divisor)

b) Next write the coefficient of the polynomial that is to be divided. The polynomial should be arranged in descending order, and in case any term is missing, use 0 in that place against the missing term.

$$\begin{array}{c|cccc} 2 & 2 & -5 & 3 & 7 \\ \hline & & & & \end{array}$$

c) Carry the first number down.

$$\begin{array}{c|cccc} 2 & 2 & -5 & 3 & 7 \\ & \downarrow & & & \\ \hline & 2 & & & \end{array}$$

d) Multiply the number carried down with the divisor and write the result in the next column.

$$\begin{array}{c|cccc} 2 & 2 & -5 & 3 & 7 \\ & \downarrow & 4 & & \\ \hline & 2 & & & \end{array}$$

e) Add the number in the second column and write the result at the bottom.

$$\begin{array}{c|cccc} 2 & 2 & -5 & 3 & 7 \\ & \downarrow & 4 & & \\ \hline & 2 & -1 & & \end{array}$$

f) Multiply the second number in the column by the divisor and write it below in the next column.

$$\begin{array}{c|cccc} 2 & 2 & -5 & 3 & 7 \\ & \downarrow & 4 & -2 & \\ \hline & 2 & -1 & & \end{array}$$

g) Now add the two numbers of the third column and write the result below.

$$\begin{array}{r|rrrr} 2 & 2 & -5 & 3 & 7 \\ & \downarrow & 4 & -2 & \\ \hline & 2 & -1 & 1 \end{array}$$

h) Multiply the third number in the bottom line with the divisor and write the product in the fourth column.

$$\begin{array}{r|rrrr} 2 & 2 & -5 & 3 & 7 \\ & \downarrow & 4 & -2 & 2 \\ \hline & 2 & -1 & 1 \end{array}$$

i) Add the two numbers in the fourth column.

$$\begin{array}{r|rrrr} 2 & 2 & -5 & 3 & 7 \\ & \downarrow & 4 & -2 & 2 \\ \hline & 2 & -1 & 1 & ⑨ \end{array}$$

The division is complete. The last digit of the bottom line which is encircled is the remainder. Now you can write the result. The bottom line gives us the quotient and the remainder together. In order to write the quotient, diminish one power of the polynomial and place it with each term from the left-most digit to the right. The power of the number should also be written in descending order.

Dividend = $2x^3 - 5x^2 + 3x + 7$

Divisor = $x - 2$

Quotient = $2x^2 - x + 1$

Remainder = 9

The best thing about this method is how simple it is. There is no need to worry about subtraction, tough multiplication and arrangement of power. Isn't it simple?

Example 2: Let $p(x) = 2x^3 - 5x + 3$

a)   Find the remainder when it is divided by $x + 2$

b)   Check whether $x = 1$ is a zero of p

[Zero of a polynomial means if you put that value in the polynomial then it will have zero as remainder.

$p(x) = 2x^3 - 5x + 3$

$p(1) = 2 - 5 + 3 = 0$]

Solution: As stated above, first write the polynomials in decreasing order of their power.

$p(x) = 2x^3 + 0x^2 - 5x + 3$

Now write the coefficient in decreasing order and place $x = -2$ in the divisor column as shown.

$-2 \mid 2 \quad 0 \quad -5 \quad 3$

Now, carry down the first number and write it below the line. Multiply it with the divisor and place the result $2 \times -2 = -4$ below 0 in the dividend column. Add the result of the second column and write it below the line.

$0 + (-4) = -4$

Multiply it again with the divisor.

$-4 \times -2 = 8.$

Repeat the same process.

$$
\begin{array}{r|rrrr}
-2 & 2 & 0 & -5 & 3 \\
   & \downarrow & -4 & 8 & -6 \\
\hline
   & 2 & -4 & 3 & \boxed{-3}
\end{array}
$$

Therefore, Quotient $= 2x^2 - 4x + 3$

Remainder $= -3$

Example 3: Divide $x^3 + 6x^2 + 11x + 6$ by $x + 3$

Solution: Here, I shall only focus on single step division as everything has been well explained in the above example.

First put x + 3 = 0 to get the digit to be placed in the divisor column.

$\Rightarrow$x + 3 = 0

$\Rightarrow$x = − 3

Place the coefficients of the polynomial − 1, 6, 11 and 6 in the dividend column.

$$\underline{-3}\,\Big|\; 1 \quad 6 \quad 11 \quad 6$$

Now carry the first digit down. Multiply it by the divisor and place it in the next column.

1 × − 3 = − 3

Add the second column.

6 + (− 3) = 3

Multiply the digit placed at the bottom of the second column by the divisor and place it below the third column.

3 × − 3 = − 9

Add the digits in the third column.

$$\begin{array}{r|rrrr}
-3 & 1 & 6 & 11 & 6 \\
   & \downarrow & -3 & -9 & -6 \\
\hline
   & 1 & 3 & 2 \;| & 0
\end{array}$$

Example 4: Divide $2x^3 + 5x^2 + 9$ by x + 3.

Solution: Put x + 3 = 0

$\Rightarrow$ x = − 3

Arrange the dividend in descending order of power.

$2x^3 + 5x^2 + 0x + 9$

Now place the coefficient of the dividend and the divisor as shown here:

$$-3 \mid \quad 2 \quad 5 \quad 0 \quad 9$$

Carry down the first digit (2) and multiply it by the divisor
(– 3) and place the result (2 × – 3 = – 6) in the next column.

$$-3 \mid \quad 2 \quad \quad 5 \quad \quad 0 \quad \quad 9$$
$$\downarrow \quad -6$$
$$2$$

Add the digit in the second column and write the result
(5 – 6 = – 1) below. Multiply it again with the divisor and
place the result (– 1 × – 3 = 3) below the third column.

Add the two digits of the third column and place the
result at the bottom.

$$-3 \mid \quad 2 \quad \quad 5 \quad \quad 0 \quad \quad 9$$
$$\downarrow \quad -6 \quad 3$$
$$2 \quad -1 \quad 3$$

Finally, multiply the result obtained in the third column by
the divisor (3 × – 3 = – 9)

$$-3 \mid \quad 2 \quad \quad 5 \quad \quad 0 \quad \quad 9$$
$$\downarrow \quad -6 \quad 3 \quad -9$$
$$2 \quad -1 \quad 3 \quad 0$$

Hence, for the polynomial

$p(x) = 2x^3 + 5x^2 + 9$

Quotient = $2x^2 - x + 3$

Remainder = 0

Let's have one more example.

Example 5: Divide $x^3 + 1 = 0$ by $x + 1$.

Solution: Here, polynomial $p(x) = x^3 + 1$.

First write the polynomials in descending order of their power.

$p(x) = x^3 + 0x^2 + 0x + 1$

Now, put $x + 1 = 0$

$\Rightarrow x = -1$

Now make a division box and place the coefficient of the polynomials in the dividend part and put -1 in the divisor part.

Hope you have understood the process described in the above examples, so here the whole process is done in a single step.

$$
\begin{array}{r|rrrr}
-1 & 1 & 0 & 0 & 1 \\
& \downarrow & -1 & 1 & -1 \\
\hline
& 1 & -1 & 1 & 0 \\
\end{array}
$$

Once the division part is complete, place the power of the variable one less than the original in the decreasing order in the answer part.

Hence, quotient $= x^2 - x + 1$.

Remainder $= 0$

Example 6: Divide $x^4 + 4x^3 - 22x^2 - 4x + 21$ by $x^2 - 1$.

Solution: The divisor should be written as $x^2 + 0x - 1$.

Let's write the coefficient of the dividend and the divisor.

$$
\begin{array}{r|r|rrr|rr}
& & x^4 + 4x^3 & - 22x^2 & - 4x & + 21 & \\
\hline
0 - 1 & 1 & 4 & -22 & -4 & +21 \\
& & 0 & 1 & & \\
& & & 0 & 4 & \\
& & & & 0 & -21 \\
\hline
& 1 & 4 & -21 & 0 & 0 \\
\end{array}
$$

Dividend $= x^2 + 4x - 21$

Remainder $= 0$

Example 7: Divide $x^4 - 8x^3 + 17x^2 + 2x - 24$ by $x^2 - x - 2$.

Solution: Divisor is $x^2 - x - 2$. So, change the sign of the coefficient and the constant term and place it in the divisor column leaving the highest power. Write the coefficient of the dividend as well, and follow the previous instructions.

		$x^4 + 8x^3 - 17x^2 - 2x + 24$			
$1 - 2$	1	-8	17	2	-24
		1	2		
			-7	-14	
				12	24
	1	-7	12	0	0

Hence, Quotient $= x^2 - 7x + 12$ and Remainder $= 0$

Example 8: Divide $2x^4 + 11x^3 - 13x^2 - 99x - 45$ by $x^2 + 2x - 15$.

Solution: Place the revised divisor and coefficient of the dividend in the respective columns and do as instructed in the rule. Here, divisor is $x^2 + 2x - 15$, whose coefficient is $1 + 2 - 15$. Change the coefficient of the last two terms (leaving the coefficient of highest power).

$$\begin{array}{r|rrr|rr}
& 2x^4 + 11x^3 - 13x^2 - 99x + 45 & & & & \\
\hline
2 - 15 & 2 & 11 & -13 & -99 & -45 \\
& & -4 & 30 & & \\
& & & -14 & 105 & \\
& & & & -6 & 45 \\
\hline
& 2 & 7 & 3 & 0 & 0
\end{array}$$

Quotient $= 2x^2 + 7x + 3$

Remainder $= 0$

The division of polynomials is understood to be a difficult exercise which can be simplified using the Vedic technique in a single line or two. The more you practise, the more comfortable you will be to find the solution in seconds.

7

Linear Equations

Introduction

The word 'equation' in mathematics is a statement that asserts the equality of two expressions. There are many types of equations available in mathematics, but we shall simply focus on linear equations of different types, and quadratic equations in due course. Here we shall look at the difference between the traditional method and the Vedic method. The tediousness of the traditional method and ease of the Vedic method will help you understand the importance of Vedic Mathematics. Let's start with some examples.

Type 1: Simple equations with two variables

Example 1: $4x + 12 = 3x + 16$

Solution: First we change the position of the variables and the constant. Generally, we keep variables on the left side and constants on the right side.

$$4x + 12 = 3x + 16$$
$$\Rightarrow 4x - 3x = 16 - 12 = 4$$
$$\Rightarrow x = 4$$

Let's suppose that we have the equation

ax + b = cx + d

$$\Rightarrow x = \frac{d - b}{a - c}$$

Let's solve the same equation mentally with the above formula.

4x + 12 = 3x + 16

$$\Rightarrow x = \frac{16 - 12}{4 - 3} = 4$$

Example 2: 17x – 13 = 13x + 3

Solution:

$$x = \frac{3 + 13}{17 - 13} = 4$$

Example 3: 7x + 33 = 11x – 19

Solution:

$$x = \frac{-19 - 33}{7 - 11} = 13.5$$

Example 4: 32x + 49 = 45x – 93

Solution:

$$x = \frac{-93 - 49}{32 - 45} = \frac{-142}{-13} = \frac{142}{13}$$

Type 2: (x + m) (x + n) = (x + p) (x + q)

This is another example of the method of Paravartya Yojayet or transpose and apply. Here the left hand and right hand sides both contain binomial factors.

In this case, you first have to open the brackets of both sides and cancel out the like terms and find the value of x.

Let's do it in one line.

$$x = \frac{\text{Product of constant term of RHS} - \text{Product of constant term of LHS}}{\text{Sum of constant term of LHS} - \text{Sum of constant term of RHS}}$$

If we have

$$(x + m)(x + n) = (x + p)(x + q)$$

$$\Rightarrow x = \frac{pq - mm}{m + n - p - q}$$

Let's look at some examples.

Example 1: If $(y + 1)(y + 2) = (y + 3)(y + 4)$ then find y.

Solution: $\quad y = \dfrac{3 \times 4 - 1 \times 2}{1 + 2 - 3 - 4} = -5/2$

Example 2: $(x + 7)(x + 9) = (x + 3)(x + 21)$

Solution: $\quad x = \dfrac{63 - 63}{7 + 9 - 3 - 21} = 0$

Example 3: $(z - 1)(z - 2) = (z - 3)(z - 4)$

Solution: $\quad x = \dfrac{12 - 2}{-1 - 2 + 3 + 4} = 10/4$

Example 4: $(p - a)(p - b) = (p + c)(p - d)$

Solution: $\quad p = \dfrac{-cd - ab}{-a - b - c + d} = \dfrac{cd + ab}{a + b + c - d}$

Type 3:

$$p = \frac{ax + b}{cx + d} = \frac{p}{q}$$

This is one of the examples where we do a transposition and find the value of x. Some practice will help you to do the whole calculation mentally.

If we have $\dfrac{ax + b}{cx + d} = \dfrac{p}{q}$

Then $x = \dfrac{pd - bq}{aq - cp}$

Example 1: If $\dfrac{2x - 7}{5x - 9} = \dfrac{4}{7}$ then find x.

Solution: Here a = 2, b = 7, c = 5, d = – 9, p = 4 and q = 7.

$$\Rightarrow x = \frac{-36 - 49}{14 - 20}$$

$$= \frac{-85}{-6} = \frac{85}{6}$$

Example 2: Solve $\dfrac{x - 5}{3x + 2} = \dfrac{2}{23}$

Solution: $x = \dfrac{4 + 115}{23 - 6} = \dfrac{119}{17} = 7$

Example 3: Solve the equation $\dfrac{5x + 19}{2x - 7} = \dfrac{11}{9}$

Solution: $x = \dfrac{-77 - 119}{45 - 22} = \dfrac{196}{23}$

Type 4:

$$\frac{m}{x + a} + \frac{n}{x + b} = 0$$

This is the fourth type of linear equation in one variable. Basically, you need to take the Lowest Common Multiple (LCM) of the denominator and solve it to get the value of x, but if you remember the one line formula, then you can do it instantly.

For the above equation,

$$x = \frac{-mb - na}{m + n}$$

Example 1: Solve for x:

$$\frac{2}{x + 3} + \frac{5}{x + 7} = 0$$

Solution: Here, m = 2, n = 5, a = 3 and b = 7

$$x = \frac{-mb + na}{m + n} = \frac{-14 - 15}{2 + 5} = \frac{-29}{7}$$

Example 2: Solve for x:

$$\frac{1}{x + 3} + \frac{7}{x + 11} = 0$$

Solution: m = 1, n = 7, a = 3 and b = 11

Hence, $x = \dfrac{-11 - 21}{1 + 7} = -4$

Example 3: Solve for y:

$$\frac{3}{y + 15} + \frac{7}{y - 19} = 0$$

Solution: m = 3, n = 7, a = 15 and b = – 19

Hence, $y = \dfrac{\mp 57 - 105}{3 + 7} = \dfrac{-105}{10} = 10.5$

Type 5:

$$(x + a)\,(x + b) = (x + c)\,(x + d)$$

In this type of equation, if the product of the constant term of one side is equal to that of the other side, then the variable value always comes out to be 0.

Example 1: (x + 5) (x + 8) = (x + 4) (x + 10)

Solution: Product of constant term of LHS = 40 = Product of constant term of RHS

Hence, x = 0

Example 2: (p – 9) (p – 8) = (p – 18) (p – 4)

Solution: Product of constant term of LHS = 72 = Product of constant term of RHS

Hence, p = 0

Type 6:

$$\frac{p}{(x + a)\,(x + b)} + \frac{q}{(x + b)\,(x + c)} \; \frac{r}{(x + c)\,(x + c)} = 0$$

This type of equation at first glance looks daunting, but the Paravartya Yojayet Vedic sutra turns this into a one-line solution.

$$x = \frac{\text{Each N multiplied by the absent number with sign reversed}}{\text{Sum of all numerators}}$$

Example 1:

$$\frac{1}{(x+2)\ (x+3)} + \frac{3}{(x+3)\ (x+5)}\ \frac{2}{(x+5)\ (x+2)} = 0$$

Solution: Here we can see the denominator has three terms $(x+2)$, $(x+3)$ and $(x+5)$.

$$x = \frac{1 \times -5 + 3 \times -2 + 2 \times -3}{1+2+3} = \frac{-5-6-6}{6} = \frac{-17}{6}$$

Example 2:

$$\frac{1}{(x+3)\ (x+4)} + \frac{3}{(x-4)\ (x-9)} + \frac{5}{(x-9)\ (x-3)} = 0$$

Solution: Here we can see the denominator has three terms, $(x-3)$, $(x-4)$ and $(x-9)$.

$$x = \frac{1 \times 9 + 3 \times 3 + 5 \times 4}{1+3+5} = \frac{38}{9}$$

Example 3: Solve the given equation.

$$\frac{1}{x^2 + 3x + 2} + \frac{5}{x^2 + 5x + 6} + \frac{3}{x^2 + 4x + 3} = 0$$

Solution: Factorizing the denominator, we get

$$\frac{1}{(x+1)(x+2)} + \frac{5}{(x+2)(x \mp 3)} + \frac{3}{(x+1)(x+3)} = 0$$

Hence,

$$x = \frac{1 \times -3 + 5 \times -1 + 3 \times -2}{1 + 5 + 3} = \frac{-3 - 5 - 6}{9} = \frac{-14}{9}$$

Besides that, there are other types of equations that we will explore in the next chapter, so be ready to delve into the quadratic equation, an equation that has 2 as the highest degree of the variable.

8

Linear Equations in Two Variables

Introduction

Two linear equations using two unknown variables x and y are said to form a system of simultaneous equations, if each of them is satisfied by the same pair of values for x and y.

Example: $x + y = 4$ and $x - y = 3$ is an example of a simultaneous equation.

The basic concept of such equations is the backbone of algebra, and it is introduced in the NCERT syllabus in Class X. There are many methods to arrive at the answer, and we generally follow the four methods that are part of our curriculum. They are:

a) Method of Elimination
b) Method of Comparison
c) Method of Substitution
d) Method of Cross Multiplication

The Vedic method is fast and simple. It makes calculation easy and far quicker than the traditional methods. The most important feature of Vedic mathematics is its various techniques to help solve problems in no time, using easy and convenient methods.

VEDIC SUTRAS FOR SOLVING
SIMULTANEOUS EQUATIONS

Meaning of Vedic Sutra

1. **Paravartya Yojayet:** The literal meaning of this sutra is: 'Transpose and Apply'. The well-known rule relating to transposition enjoins an invariable change of sign with every change in side.
2. **Anurupye Sunyamanyat:** The sutra says, 'if one is in ratio, the other one is 0'. A detailed explanation with examples is given below.
3. **Sankalana–vyavakalana-bhyam:** This sutra has also been used in the chapter on subtraction. The simple meaning of the sutra is 'addition and subtraction'.

Paravartya Yojayet

This method is applicable for all sorts of linear simultaneous equations. The cross multiplication method taught in our present-day curriculum is somewhat akin to the Paravartya sutra. The Vedic sutra moves in a cyclic order.

For x, we start with the y coefficient and the independent terms and cross multiply them in the forward direction. The sign between the two cross multiplications is a minus.

For y, we start with the independent term and x coefficients and cross multiply them in the backward direction. The sign between the cross multiplication results is a minus.

For the result of the denominator, we take the coefficient of variables only, and cross multiply them in a backward direction.

Suppose we have the following set of simultaneous equations:

$$a_1x + b_1y = c_1$$
$$a_2x + b_2y = c_2$$

In order to get the numerator of x, we leave the coefficient of x and write the coefficient of y and the independent term and cross multiply them in the rightward direction with a minus sign in between the cross products, as shown here.

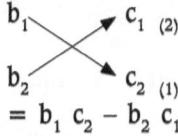

$$= b_1\ c_2 - b_2\ c_1$$

Again, to get the numerator of y, we leave the coefficient of y and take only the coefficient of x and the independent term into consideration. As you know, the sutra moves in a cyclic order, so we have to start with the independent term first. Cross multiplication of the independent term and the coefficient of x will give the numerator of y.

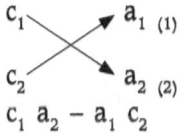

$$c_1\ a_2 - a_1\ c_2$$

The denominators of both the variables x and y will remain the same. The cross products of the coefficients of the variables in the backward direction gives us the result:

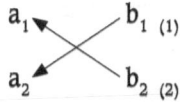

To make the concept even more clear, let us put the whole thing in a simple diagrammatic structure.

Numerator of x   Numerator of y   Denominator (for x and y)

Let us look at a few examples to understand the modus operandi.

Example 1: Solve for x and y:

$$2x + 3y = 7; \; 3x + 7y = 13.$$

Solution:

Hence,

$$x = \frac{39 - 49}{9 - 14} = \frac{-10}{-5} = 2$$

$$y = \frac{21 - 26}{9 - 14} = \frac{-5}{-5} = 1$$

Now let's simplify the solution part.

Suppose we have two equations:

ax + by = c

dx + ey = f

then $x = \dfrac{bf - ce}{bd - ae}$ and $y = \dfrac{cd - af}{bd - ae}$

Example 2: Solve for x and y:

11x + 6y = 21

8x − 5y = 34.

Solution:

Here, a = 11, b = 6, c = 21

d = 8, e = − 5 and f = 34

$x = \dfrac{bf - ce}{bd - ae} = \dfrac{6 \times 34 - 21 \times -5}{6 \times 8 - 11 \times -5} = 3$ and $y = \dfrac{cd - af}{bd - ae} = \dfrac{21 \times 8 - 11 \times 34}{6 \times 8 - 11 \times -5} - 2$

Example 3: Solve for x and y:

4x + 7y = 29

12x + 3y = − 3

Solution: Here, a = 4, b = 7 and c = 29

d = 12, e = 3 and f = − 3

$x = \dfrac{bf - ce}{bd - ae} = \dfrac{7 \times -3 - 29 \times 3}{7 \times 12 - 4 \times 3} = -1.5$ and $y = \dfrac{cd - af}{bd - ae} = \dfrac{29 \times 12 - 4 \times -3}{7 \times 12 - 4 \times -3} = 5$

Anurupye Sunyamanyat

This Vedic sutra says, 'if one is in ratio, the other one is 0'. In simple language, whenever the ratio of x or y is equal to that of the independent term, put the ratio of y or x = 0.

This is a special type of linear equation which can be

solved using the Vedic technique in a few seconds.

Let us look at a few examples to make the modus operandi understandable.

Example 1: Solve for x and y:

$$5x + 8y = 40$$
$$10x + 11y = 80$$

Solution: In the above example, the ratio of the coefficients of x is 1:2 and the ratio of the independent terms is also 1:2. The Vedic sutra in this special case says that if one is in ratio, the other one is 0.

Since the ratio of x is equal to the ratio of the independent terms, y = 0. Put y = 0 in either of the equations to get the value of x.

For y = 0, 10x = 80, hence x = 8

x = 8 and y = 0 is the solution.

Example 2: Solve for x and y:

$$12x + 78y = 12$$
$$16x + 96y = 16$$

Solution: Here the ratio of x = 12:16 = ratio of the independent terms

Hence, y = 0

Put y = 0 in either of the two equations to get x = 1

Example 3: Solve for x and y:

$$44x + 178y = 22$$
$$132x + 243y = 66$$

Solution: Here the ratio of coefficients of x = 44:132 = 1:3

The ratio of the independent terms = 22:66 = 1:3

Hence, y = 0

Put y = 0 to get x = ½

Example 4: Solve for x and y:
$$3x + 5y = 8$$
$$7x + 15y = 24$$

Solution: As you can see, the ratio of the coefficients of y = 5:15 = 1:3 which is the same as the ratio of the constant terms = 8:24 = 1:3

Hence, x = 0

Put the value of x in any equation and you get y = 8/5

Example 5: Solve for x and y:
$$27x + 144y = 720$$
$$42x + 72y = 360$$

Solution: Here the ratio of coefficients of y = 144:72 = 2:1
The ratio of independent terms = 720:360 = 2:1
Hence, x = 0
Put x = 0 in any of the above equation to get y = 5.

Example 6: Solve for x and y:
$$2a - 14b = 14$$
$$381a - 267b = 267$$

Solution: Minute observation explains the result.
Ratio of coefficients of b = 14:267
Ratio of independent terms = 14:267
Hence, a = 0 and b = -1

Sankalana Vyavakalanam

As mentioned earlier, this sutra simply means addition and subtraction. Whenever the coefficient of x in the first equation is equal to the coefficient of y in the second equation and vice versa, this sutra works better.

Let us look at an example and see its modus operandi.

Example 1: Solve for x and y:
$$23x + 31y = 18$$
$$31x + 23y = 90$$

Solution: In the above example

The coefficient of x in 1st equation = Coefficient of y in 2nd equation = 23

The coefficient of y in 1st equation = coefficient of x in 2nd equation = 31

Let us apply the Sankalana Vyavkalanam Vedic sutra to get a quick answer.

Adding the two equations, we get $54x + 54y = 108 \Rightarrow x + y = 2$ ...(A)

On subtracting, we get $-8x + 8y = -72$, $\Rightarrow -x + y = -9$ ...(B)

Add equation (A) and (B) to get $y = -7/2$

On subtracting equations (A) and (B) again, we get $x = 1/2$

Example 2: Solve for x and y:
$$45x - 23y = 113$$
$$23x - 45y = 91$$

Solution: We have
$$45x - 23y = 113 \quad ...(1)$$
$$23x - 45y = 91 \quad ...(2)$$

Adding (1) and (2), we get $68x - 68y = 204 \Rightarrow x - y = 3$ ...(3)

Subtracting (2) from (1), we get $22x + 22y = 22 \Rightarrow x + y = 1$ ...(4)

Again, on adding equations (3) and (4), we get x = 2

And on subtracting (4) from (3), we get y = – 1

Example 3: Solve for x and y:

$$699x + 845y = 5477$$
$$845x + 699y = 5331$$

Solution: We have

$$699x + 845y = 5477 \text{ ...(1)}$$
$$845x + 699y = 5331 \text{ ...(2)}$$

Add (1) and (2) $\Rightarrow$ 1544x + 1544y = 10808 $\Rightarrow$ x + y = 7 ...(3)

Subtracting (2) from (1), we get – 146x + 146y = 146 $\Rightarrow$ – x + y = 1 ...(4)

Adding (3) and (4), we get y = 4

Subtracting (4) from (3), we get x = 3

Example 4: Solve for x and y:

$$23x - 29y = 98$$
$$29x - 23y = 110$$

Solution: We have

$$23x - 29y = 98 \text{ ...(1)}$$
$$29x - 23y = 110 \text{ ...(2)}$$

Adding (1) and (2), we get 52x – 52y = 208 $\Rightarrow$ x – y = 4 ...(3)

Subtracting (2) from (1) we have, – 6x – 6y = – 12 $\Rightarrow$ x + y = 2 ...(4)

Add (3) and (4) again to get x = 3

Subtract (4) from (3) and get y = 1

Example 5: Solve for x and y:

$$41x + 53y = 135$$
$$53x + 41y = 147$$

Solution: Adding, we get $94x + 94y = 282 \Rightarrow x + y = 3$

On subtracting, $-12x + 12y = -12 \Rightarrow -x + y = -1$

Solving these two reduced equations we have

$X = 2$ and $y = 1$

Example 6: Solve for x and y:

$$5m + 4n = 220$$
$$4m + 5n = 230$$

Solution: On adding the two equations, we get

$9m + 9n = 450 \Rightarrow m + n = 50$ ...(a)

On subtracting the two equations, we get

$$m - n = -10 \text{ ...(b)}$$

Solving (a) and (b), we get

$m = 20$ and $n = 30$

You can see what an important role Vedic Mathematics can play in reducing the time of solving two linear equations with two variables. The message is clear, through these examples, that Vedic Mathematics may prove to be a boon if it is adopted in the present day curriculum.

9

Quadratic Equations

Introduction

An equation in the form of $ax^2 + bx + c = 0$ is called a quadratic equation, where $a \neq 0$.

The fundamental theorem of algebra says that **every polynomial of m degree has m roots.** Since the degree of a quadratic equation is 2, it will have two roots. The quadratic equation $ax^2 + bx + c = 0$ is solved by the formula

$$x = \frac{-b \pm \sqrt{b^2 - 4ac}}{2a}$$

where $D = b^2 - 4ac$ is called the Discriminant. This Discriminant also helps us to decide the nature of roots of the equation. There are different methods to solve such equations:

a) Mid-term factorization
b) Completing the square method
c) Quadratic formula

These are the Vedic methods to solve quadratic equations:

1. **Vilokanam:** The literal meaning of the Sanskrit word Vilokanam is 'by observation'. There are many quadratic

problems that can be solved by minute observation. Vilokanam sutra will help you to observe minutely and give you the answers to some specific quadratic problems in seconds.

2. **Sunyam Samya Samuccaya:** This sutra is applicable to a large number of different cases. It literally means, 'when the samuccaya is the same, equal it to zero'. Samuccaya is a technical term that has different meanings under different contexts and we shall explain them one at a time.

3. **Anurupye Sunyamanyat:** This sutra is useful in finding one root of a quadratic equation of a special type. The literal meaning is, 'if one is in ratio, the other one is zero'. It has many other applications in Vedic Mathematics.

Vilokanam Sutra

'Vilokanama' means 'only by observation'. The tough-looking quadratic equation below can be solved in a few seconds using the Vedic method, whereas the traditional method takes at least five minutes to solve.

Example: $\dfrac{x + 2}{x + 1} + \dfrac{x + 1}{x + 2} = \dfrac{37}{6}$

Traditional Method:

Put $\dfrac{x + 2}{x + 1} = a$

Hence,

$a + 1/a = 37/6$

or, $\dfrac{a^2 + 1}{a} = \dfrac{37}{6}$

or, $6a^2 + 6 = 37a$

or, $6a^2 - 37a + 6 = 0$

or, $6a^2 - 36a - a + 6 = 0$

or, $6a(a - 6) - 1 (a - 6) = 0$

or, $(6a - 1) (a - 6) = 0$

or, $a = 6$ or $1/6$

Now,

$\dfrac{x + 2}{x + 1} = 6$ or, $\dfrac{x + 2}{x + 1} = \dfrac{1}{6}$

$\Rightarrow 6x + 6 = x + 2$ $\qquad\qquad \Rightarrow 6x + 12 = x + 1$

$\Rightarrow 6x - x = 2 - 6$ $\qquad\qquad \Rightarrow 6x - x = 1 - 12$

$\Rightarrow 5x = -4$ $\qquad\qquad\qquad \Rightarrow 5x = -11$

$\Rightarrow x = -4/5$ $\qquad\qquad\qquad \Rightarrow x = -11/5$

Vedic method:

Look at the LHS; you observe that it is the sum of two reciprocals. The Vilokanam Vedic sutra simply tells us to break the RHS in such a way that it becomes the sum of two reciprocals, and then equate both the terms of the RHS to any term of the LHS. Let us understand the modus operandi with these examples.

Example 1: Solve $\dfrac{x + 2}{x + 1} + \dfrac{x + 1}{x + 2} = \dfrac{37}{6}$

Solution: The LHS is the sum of two reciprocals, so we break the RHS into two such fractions that it also becomes the sum of two reciprocal fractions.

$$\frac{x+2}{x+1} + \frac{x+1}{x+2} = \frac{37}{6} = \frac{6+1}{6}$$

Now, equate either of the LHS terms to both the terms of the RHS and solve the equations to find the values of x.

$$\frac{x+2}{x+1} = 6 \qquad \text{or,} \quad \frac{x+2}{x+1} = \frac{1}{6}$$

$\Rightarrow 6x + 6 = x + 2$ $\qquad\qquad \Rightarrow 6x + 12 = x + 1$

$\Rightarrow 6x - x = 2 - 6$ $\qquad\qquad \Rightarrow 6x - x = 1 - 12$

$\Rightarrow 5x = -4$ $\qquad\qquad\qquad \Rightarrow 5x = -11$

$\Rightarrow x = -4/5$ $\qquad\qquad\qquad \Rightarrow x = -11/5$

Example 2: $x + 1/x = 26/5$

Solution: $\quad x + \dfrac{1}{x} = 5\dfrac{1}{5}$

$\qquad\qquad \Rightarrow x = 5$ or $1/5$

Example 3: $(x-5) + \dfrac{1}{x-5} = \dfrac{5}{6}$

Solution: $(x-5) + \dfrac{1}{x-5} = \dfrac{5}{6} = \dfrac{3}{2} - \dfrac{2}{3}$

Comparing, we get

$x - 5 = \dfrac{3}{2}$ or $-\dfrac{2}{3}$

$\Rightarrow x = \dfrac{13}{2}$ or $\dfrac{13}{3}$

Example 4: Solve $\dfrac{x+2}{x+3} - \dfrac{x+3}{x+2} = \dfrac{15}{4}$

Solution: The LHS is the difference of two reciprocals, so we break the RHS into two such fractions so that it also becomes the difference of two reciprocal fractions.

$$\frac{x+2}{x+3} - \frac{x+3}{x+2} = \frac{15}{4} = \frac{4-1}{4}$$

Now equate either of the LHS terms to both the terms of the RHS and solve the equations to find the values of x.

$\dfrac{x+2}{x+3} = 4$ or, $\dfrac{x+2}{x+3} = \dfrac{1}{4}$

$\Rightarrow 4x + 12 = x + 2$ $4x + 8 = x + 3$

$\Rightarrow 4x - x = 2 - 12$ $4x - x = 3 - 8$

$\Rightarrow 3x = -10$ $3x = -5$

$\Rightarrow x = -10/3$ $x = -5/3$

Example 5: Solve $\dfrac{x}{x+1} + \dfrac{x+1}{x} = \dfrac{169}{60}$

Solution: The LHS is the sum of two reciprocals, so we break the RHS into two such fractions so that it also becomes the sum of two reciprocal fractions. At first glance, the RHS doesn't seem to be the sum of any such fraction.

Now split the denominator into two parts.

$60 = 2 \times 30$

   $= 3 \times 20$

   $= 4 \times 15$

   $= 5 \times 12$

   $= 6 \times 10$

Now find the sum of the squares of these factors and check when the sum is 169, the value of the numerator.

$2^2 + 30^2 > 169$

$3^2 + 20^2 > 169$

$4^2 + 15^2 > 169$

But $52 + 122 = 169$ (Numerator)

Hence, $169/60 = 12/5 + 5/12$

$$\frac{x}{x+1} + \frac{x+1}{x} = \frac{169}{60} = \frac{12}{5} + \frac{5}{12}$$

Now, equate either of the LHS terms to both the terms of the RHS, and solve the equations to find the values of x.

$$\frac{x}{x+1} = \frac{12}{5}$$

$\Rightarrow 12x + 12 = 5x$

$\Rightarrow 12x - 5x = -12$

$\Rightarrow 7x = -12$

$\Rightarrow x = -12/7$

or, $\dfrac{x}{x+1} = \dfrac{5}{12}$

$\Rightarrow 12x = 5x + 5$

$\Rightarrow 12x - 5x = 5$

$\Rightarrow 7x = 5$

$\Rightarrow x = 5/7$

Example 6: Solve $\dfrac{3x+7}{2x-9} - \dfrac{2x+9}{3x+7} = \dfrac{56}{45}$

Solution: The LHS is the difference of two reciprocals, so we break the RHS into two such fractions that it also becomes the difference of two reciprocal fractions. At first look, the RHS doesn't seem to be the sum of any such fraction. Now split the denominator into two parts.

$$45 = 3 \times 15$$
$$= 9 \times 5$$

Now find the difference of squares of these factors and check when the difference is found to be 56, the value of the numerator.

152 − 32 > 56

But 92 − 52 = 56 (Numerator)

Hence, $\dfrac{56}{45} = \dfrac{9}{5} - \dfrac{5}{9}$

The equation now becomes:

$$\frac{3x + 7}{2x - 9} - \frac{2x + 9}{3x + 7} = \frac{56}{45} = \frac{9}{5} - \frac{5}{9}$$

Now, equate either of the LHS terms to both the terms of the RHS and solve the equations to find the values of x.

$\dfrac{3x + 7}{2x + 9} = \dfrac{9}{5}$	or, $\dfrac{3x + 7}{2x - 9} = \dfrac{5}{9}$
$\Rightarrow 15x + 35 = 18x - 81$	$\Rightarrow 27x + 63 = 10x - 45$
$\Rightarrow 15x - 18x = -81 - 35$	$\Rightarrow 27x - 10x = -45 - 63$
$\Rightarrow -3x = -116$	$\Rightarrow 17x = -108$
$\Rightarrow x = 116/3$	$\Rightarrow x = -108/17$

Sunyam Anyat and Sunyam Sama Samuccaya

Let us look at the following examples:

a) $\dfrac{2}{x + 2} + \dfrac{3}{x + 3} = \dfrac{4}{x + 4} + \dfrac{1}{x + 1}$

b) $\dfrac{a + b}{x + a + b} + \dfrac{b + c}{x + b + c} = \dfrac{2b}{x + 2b} + \dfrac{a + c}{x + a + c}$

Minute observation reveals the above equations to be quadratic equations, so it will certainly have two roots. The above type of equations can be solved by using two Vedic sutras.

Let us look at each example and solve it by using Vedic sutras.

a) $$\frac{2}{x+2} + \frac{3}{x+3} = \frac{4}{x+4} + \frac{1}{x+1}$$

Now let us inspect it by using **Sunyam Anyat** Vedic sutra which was earlier used in solving a special type of simultaneous equation.

The formula says, if one is in ratio, the other one is zero.

Ratio of the constant terms in LHS = 2/2 + 3/3 = 1 + 1 = 2

Ratio of the constant terms in RHS = 4/4 + 1/1 = 1 + 1 = 2

Since the ratios of the constant terms on both sides are equal, by Sunyam Anyat sutra x = 0.

Now what about the second root?

The second root will be extracted by using another Vedic sutra called **Sunyam Sama Samuccaya**. The sutra says that if the sum of the numerators on both the sides are the same, equate the sum of the denominators to zero.

$N_1 + N_2$ in LHS = 2 + 3 = 5
$N_1 + N_2$ in RHS = 4 + 1 = 5

Since they are equal, we have to equate the sum of the denominators to zero.

$$D1 + D2 = 0$$
$$\Rightarrow x + 2 + x + 3 = 0$$
$$\Rightarrow 2x + 5 = 0$$
$$\Rightarrow x = -5/2$$

Therefore, the two roots are x = 0 and x = – 5/2

Example 1: $$\frac{a+b}{x+a+b} + \frac{b+c}{x+b+c} = \frac{2b}{x+2b} + \frac{a+c}{x+a+c}$$

Solution:
Ratio of constant term in LHS = $\dfrac{a+b}{a+b} + \dfrac{b+c}{b+c} = 1 + 1 = 2$

Ratio of constant term in RHS = $\dfrac{2b}{2b} + \dfrac{a+c}{a+c} = 1 + 1 = 2$

Since the ratio of LHS and RHS are the same, $x = 0$ (by Sunyam Anyat Vedic sutra). The second root will be extracted using another Vedic sutra, Sunyam Sama Samuccaya.

$N_1 + N_2$ in LHS $= a + b + b + c = a + 2b + c$

$N_1 + N_2$ in RHS $= 2b + a + c = a + 2b + c$

Since they are equal, we have to equate the sum of the denominators to zero.

$D_1 + D_2 = 0$

$\Rightarrow x + a + b + x + b + c = 0$

$\Rightarrow 2x + a + 2b + c = 0$

$\Rightarrow x = -(a + 2b + c)/2$

Hence, the two roots are $x = 0$ and $x = -(a + 2b + c)/2$

Example 2: $\dfrac{1}{4x+5} + \dfrac{1}{5x-7} = \dfrac{1}{x-5} + \dfrac{1}{2x-17}$

Solution: Let's first transpose the negative terms of each side to the other.

Here, the sums of the denominators on both sides are the same, so we can equate the sum to zero.

$D_1 + D_2 = 0$

$\Rightarrow 4x + 5 + 2x - 17 = 0$

$\Rightarrow 6x = 12$

$\Rightarrow x = 2$

Hence, two roots are $x = 0, 2$

Sunyam Sama Samuccaya

The third case is an example of a simple quadratic equation. The traditional method is cumbersome but the Vedic method is a one line solution and does not even require pen and paper. You will be amazed to see how effective this method is. This special type of equation can be identified by summing up the numerators and denominators on both the sides. If they are found to be equal, then Sunyam Sama Samuccaya Vedic sutra will be applicable in such a case.

$N_1 + N_2 = D_1 + D_2 = 0$ gives the first root of the equation and $N_1 - D_1 = N_2 - D_2 = 0$ gives the second root of the equation

Example 1: Solve $\dfrac{3x + 4}{6x + 7} = \dfrac{5x + 6}{2x + 3}$

Solution: Upon minutely observing the question, help identify that this question falls in a special category of quadratic equations, where the sum of the numerator and denominator is found to be equal to $8x + 10$.

For the first root

$N_1 + N_2 = D_1 + D_2 = 0$
$N_1 + N_2 = 3x + 4 + 5x + 6 = 8x + 10$
$D_1 + D_2 = 6x + 7 + 2x + 3 = 8x + 10$
$\Rightarrow 8x + 10 = 0$
or, $x = -5/4$

For the second root

$N_1 - D_1 = N_2 - D_2 = 0$
$\Rightarrow N_1 - D_1 = 3x + 4 - 6x - 7 = 0$

$\Rightarrow -3x - 3 = 0$

$\Rightarrow x = 1$

or, $N_2 - D_2 = 5x + 6 - 2x - 3 = 0$

$\Rightarrow 3x + 3 = 0$

$\Rightarrow x = -1$

Hence, the two roots of the above equation are $x = -5/4$ and -1.

Example 2: Solve $\dfrac{3x + 6}{6x + 3} = \dfrac{5x + 4}{2x + 7}$

Solution: On simple observation, it is evident that the above equation is a quadratic equation and here, the sum of the numerator and denominator is found to be equal to $8x + 10$. We now apply the Sunyam Sama Samuccaya sutra to obtain the two roots of the quadratic equation.

For the first root

$N_1 + N_2 = D_1 + D_2 = 0$

$N_1 + N_2 = 3x + 6 + 5x + 4 = 8x + 10$

$D_1 + D_2 = 6x + 3 + 2x + 7 = 8x + 10$

$\Rightarrow 8x + 10 = 0$

or, $x = -5/4$

For the second root

$N_1 - D_1 = N_2 - D_2 = 0$

$\Rightarrow N_1 - D_1 = 3x + 6 - 6x - 3 = 0$

$\Rightarrow -3x + 3 = 0$

$\Rightarrow x = 1$

or, $N_2 - D_2 = 5x + 4 - 2x - 7 = 0$

$\Rightarrow 3x - 3 = 0$

$\Rightarrow x = 1$

Hence, the two roots of the above equation are
x = – 5/4 and 1.

Example 3: Solve $\dfrac{3m + 2}{2m + 3} = \dfrac{2m + 5}{3m + 4}$

Solution: Since $N_1 + N_2 = D_1 + D_2 = 5m + 7$
First root = 5m + 7 = 0
$$\Rightarrow m = -7/5$$

Second root = $N_1 - D_1 = 0$
$$\Rightarrow 3m + 2 - 2m - 3 = 0$$
$$\Rightarrow m = 1$$

Complex-looking quadratic problems that take several minutes to solve using traditional methods can be solved in a few seconds using Vedic techniques. The complexity of the calculations required to reach the answer gets reduced by practising a little. If a quadratic problem takes at least five minutes to solve using traditional methods, it can be solved without pen and paper, merely by observation, using the Vedic technique. The more you solve such problems, the more affinity you will have with Vedic techniques. So keep trying to observe the patterns, to find answers to quadratic problems in seconds.

10

Factorization of a Cubic Polynomial

Introduction

Generally, a quadratic equation is factorized by either of these three methods:

a) Completing the square
b) Mid-term factorization
c) Using the quadratic formula

But if the equation is a cubic polynomial, we don't have any short method in conventional mathematics. We do the typical factorization that involves

a) Factor Theorem method to check whether the polynomial is factorizable or not
b) Mid-term factorization method of reduced quadratic polynomial

The method discussed here is unique in the sense that it will hardly take more than thirty seconds, after sufficient practice, to crack cubic polynomials with it. Let's first understand what a Factor Theorem is.

Factor Theorem: If $p(x)$ is a polynomial, and if $p(r) = 0$, then $(x - r)$ is a factor of $p(x)$.

Example: Factorize $x^3 + 6x^2 + 11x + 6$.

Solution:

Let $p(x) = x^3 + 6x^2 + 11x + 6$.

Since 6 has the factors ± 1, ± 2, ± 3 and ± 6, we invariably put these values in the polynomial $p(x)$ until we get the remainder 0. Let us see how it works.

$p(x) = x^3 + 6x^2 + 11x + 6$

$p(1) = (1)^3 + 6(1)^2 + 11(1) + 6 \neq 0$

$p(-1) = (-1)^3 + 6(-1)^2 + 11(-1) + 6$

$\qquad = -1 + 6 - 11 + 6 = 0$

Hence $x + 1$ is a factor of the polynomial $p(x)$.

Now we divide $p(x)$ by $x + 1$ by long division method.

$$
\begin{array}{r}
x^2 + 5x + 6 \\
x + 1 \enclose{longdiv}{x^3 + 6x^2 + 11x + 6} \\
\underline{x^3 + x^2} \\
5x^2 + 11x \\
\underline{5x^2 + 5x} \\
6x + 6 \\
\underline{6x + 6} \\
\end{array}
$$

Hence, $p(x) = x^3 + 6x^2 + 11x + 6 = (x + 1)(x^2 + 5x + 6)$

Now let us factorize the polynomials $x^2 + 5x + 6$ by splitting the middle term.

$q(x) = x^2 + 5x + 6$

$\qquad = x^2 + 2x + 3x + 6$

$\qquad = x(x + 2) + 3(x + 2)$

$\qquad = (x + 2)(x + 3)$

So, $p(x) = x^3 + 6x^2 + 11x + 6$
$$= (x + 1) (x^2 + 5x + 6)$$
$$= (x + 1) (x + 2) (x + 3)$$

The above method takes a lot of time, whereas Vedic Mathematics helps you solve such problems in seconds. Let's take an example.

Vedic Method

We first begin with the sub-sutra **Gunita Samuccaya: Samuccaya Gunita** which means, 'the product of the sum of the coefficients in the factors is equal to the sum of the coefficients in the product'.

In symbols,

S_e of Product = Product of S_e (in the factor)

This sub-sutra is of immense utility for the purpose of verifying the correctness of our answer.

Example 1: $p(x) = x_3 + ax_2 + bx + c$

Solution: If the polynomial is cubic, it will have three roots—call them α, β and γ.

Hence,

$a = \alpha + \beta + \gamma$ = sum of roots = coefficient of x^2

$b = \alpha\beta + \beta\gamma + \alpha\gamma$ = sum of the product of two roots = coefficient of x

$c = \alpha\beta\gamma$ = product of three roots

Now, let's take an example to understand the effectiveness of Vedic Mathematics.

Example 2: Factorize $x^3 + 6x^2 + 11x + 6$

Solution: The last term 6 has the factors 1, 2, 3 and 6. Our aim is to find α, β and γ in such a way that it satisfies the following two conditions.

c = $\alpha\beta\gamma$ = product of three roots = $1 \times 2 \times 3$

a = $\alpha + \beta + \gamma$ = sum of roots = coefficient of x^2 = $1 + 2 + 3$

Hence the factor is $(x + 1)(x + 2)(x + 3)$

Verification:

Put the values of α, β and γ in b and check whether the coefficient of x in the polynomial is the same as the result you obtained.

b = $\alpha\beta + \beta\gamma + \alpha\gamma$ = sum of product of two = coefficient of x

$= 1 \times 2 + 2 \times 3 + 1 \times 3$

$= 2 + 6 + 3$

$= 11$

It is obvious from the result that the factor is absolutely correct.

Example 3: Factorize $x^3 - 2x^2 - 33x + 60$

Solution: The possible factors of 60 are 1, 2, 3, 4, 5, 6, 10, 12, 15, 20, 30 and 60.

a = $\alpha + \beta + \gamma$ = sum of roots = coefficient of x^2 = $- 2$

c = $\alpha\beta\gamma$ = product of three roots = 60

On simple inspection, we see:

A + $\beta + \gamma$ = sum of roots = $- 3 - 4 + 5 = - 2$

$\alpha\beta\gamma$ = product of three roots = $- 3 \times - 4 \times 5 = 60$

Hence, the factors of $x^3 - 2x^2 - 23x + 60 = (x - 3)(x - 4)(x + 5)$

Verification:

$b = \alpha\beta + \beta\gamma + \alpha\gamma$ = sum of the product of two = coefficient of x

$$= (-3) \times (-4) + (-4) \times 5 + (-3 \times 5) = -23$$

Example 4: Factorize $x^3 - 7x + 6$

Solution: This polynomial involves no term of x^2, so rewrite the equation in the standard format as discussed above.

$x^3 - 7x + 6 = x^3 + 0x^2 - 7x + 6$

Now the factors of 6 are 1, 2, 3 and 6. On inspection, we can locate the exact values of α, β and γ that suit the values of a, b and c.

$a = \alpha + \beta + \gamma$ = sum of roots = coefficient of $x^2 = 0$
$= -1 - 2 + 3$

$c = \alpha\beta\gamma$ = product of three roots $= -1 \times -2 \times 3 = 6$

Hence, $x^3 - 7x + 6 = (x - 1)(x - 2)(x + 3)$

Verification:

$b = \alpha\beta + \beta\gamma + \alpha\gamma$ = sum of product of two = coefficient of x
$= -1 \times (-2) + (-2) \times 3 + (-1) \times 3$
$= 2 - 6 - 3$
$= -7$

Hence, result verified.

Example 5: Factorize $x^3 + 13x^2 + 31x - 45$

Solution: Constant term $= -45$ and its factors are 1, 3, 5, 9, 15...

Among these factors, we have to choose three numerals whose sum is 13 and product is -45.

$13 = 9 + 5 - 1$

And $- 45 = 9 \times 5 \times - 1$

Hence,

$x^3 + 13x^2 + 31x - 45 = (x - 1)(x + 5)(x + 9)$

Verification:

We have 9, 5 and $- 1$ as its factors. Let's take two roots at a time.

$9 \times 5 + 5 \times - 1 + 9 \times - 1 = 45 - 5 - 9 = 31$

Example 6: Solve $x^3 - 10x^2 - 53x - 42$

Solution: Factors of 42 are $- 1, 2, 3, 6, 7, 14, 21...$

Among these factors, select any three such that their product is $- 42$ and sum is $- 10$.

$- 42 = 1 \times - 14 \times 3$ and

$1 \times 3 + (- 14 \times 3) + 1 \times (- 14) = 3 - 42 - 14 = - 53 =$ coefficient of x

Hence, $x^3 - 10x^2 - 53x - 42 = (x + 1)(x - 14)(x + 3)$

The above example illustrates that the Vedic method to solve the cubic factor is not only easy to understand but also a time-saving technique, because it involves no tedious or lengthy calculations but merely inspection, which helps you reach the result in no time. Always bear in mind, however, that this is only valid as long as the cubic polynomial is factorizable.

This Vedic Mathematics method of solving a cubic polynomial is the best example to show how beautiful Vedic Mathematics can be if implemented in our present-day school system. So, I urge you to keep learning Vedic Mathematics and making maths easy for yourself!

11
Combined Operations

Introduction

In traditional mathematics, we perform a single operation at a time. If you are asked to add, then you will add, and in the same way you will subtract, multiply or divide when asked to do so. Now consider a case where you have different operations to perform in a single sum. Then the traditional method fails, but Vedic Mathematics can make it easier. In a single sum, you can perform two operations at a time—addition and subtraction, multiplication and addition or multiplication and subtraction, sum of two squares or difference of two squares etc.—in a single line using the Vedic technique. Let's explore the method with some examples.

Let's first begin with the sum and difference of products.

Example: Solve 15 × 14 + 32 × 98.

Solution: In the conventional method we will first multiply 15 and 14 and then 32 and 98, and finally add the products to get the result. In Vedic Mathematics, we will work out the whole problem in three steps. But before that, you need to be familiar with the vertical and crosswise method or Urdhva Tiryagbhyam method, already discussed in detail in my previously published book, *The Essentials of Vedic Mathematics*. I am providing a brief account of this method here. I have named this method the Dot and Stick method in my book. Please check the dot operation and some examples before discussing combined operations.

Multiplication of 2-digit numbers

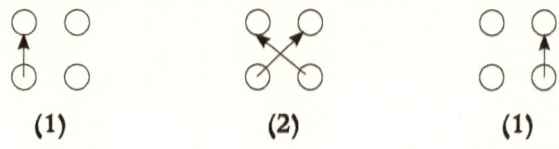

Multiplication of 3-digit numbers

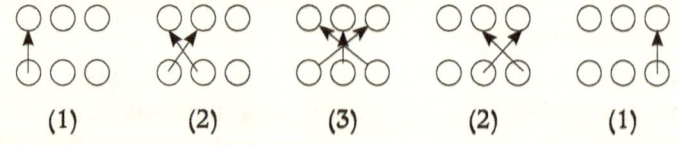

Multiplication of 4-digits numbers

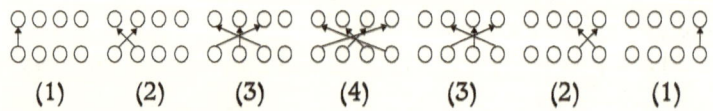

Let's take two examples.

Example 1: Multiply 76 by 42.

Solution:

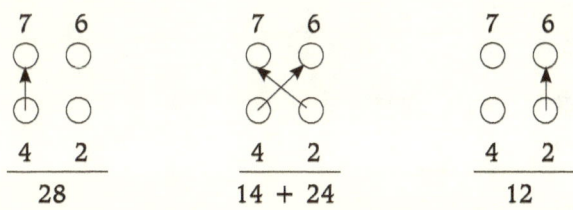

Arranging the numbers and adding them from right to left, taking only one digit at a time, we get the final result.

$$= 28 \mid 38 \mid 12$$

$$= 3192$$

Example 2: Multiply 566 by 281.

Solution:

Arrange the numbers on the dots as shown below.

Use vertical separators to separate the parts of the answer.

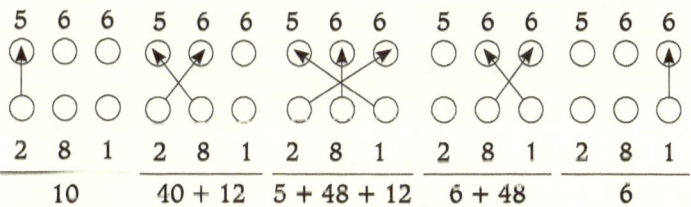

$$10 \mid 52 \mid 65 \mid 54 \mid 6$$

$$= 159046$$

Now let's go back to the question.

$$15 \times 14 + 32 \times 98$$

Step 1: $1 \times 1 + 3 \times 9 = 28$

Step 2: $1 \times 4 + 1 \times 5 + 3 \times 8 + 2 \times 9 = 51$ (cross multiplication)

Step 3: $5 \times 4 + 2 \times 8 = 36$

Arrange the result obtained in each step.

28 | 51 | 36

= 3346

Example 3: $47 \times 82 + 65 \times 94$

Solution:

Step 1: $4 \times 8 + 6 \times 9 = 32 + 54 = 86$

Step 2: $4 \times 2 + 7 \times 8 + 6 \times 4 + 5 \times 9 = 8 + 56 + 24 + 45 = 133$

Step 4: $7 \times 2 + 5 \times 4 = 14 + 20 = 34$

Arrange the results obtained with the help of separators.

86 | 133 | 34

= 86 + 13 | 3 + 3 | 4

= 9964

Example 4: Solve $44 \times 55 - 12 \times 56$

Solution:

Step 1: $-4 \times 5 - 1 \times 5 = 15$

Step 2: $4 \times 5 + 4 \times 5 - 1 \times 6 - 2 \times 5 = 24$

Step 3: $4 \times 5 - 2 \times 6 = 8$

Arrange the results obtained with the help of separators.

= 15 | 24 | 8

= 15 + 2 | 4 | 8

= 1748

Example 5: $26 \times 87 - 11 \times 34$

Solution:

Step 1: $2 \times 8 - 1 \times 3 = 13$

Step 2: $2 \times 7 + 6 \times 8 - 1 \times 4 - 1 \times 3 = 55$

Step 3: $6 \times 7 - 1 \times 4 = 38$

Arrange the results obtained with the help of separators.

$= 13 \mid 55 \mid 38$

$= 13 + 5 \mid 5 + 3 \mid 8$

$= 1888$

Sum of squares

The best method of squaring is called Duplex method in Vedic Mathematics. You can learn about Duplex in detail in my book, *The Essentials of Vedic Mathematics*. You need to understand how the Duplex method works in brief.

- Duplex of 1-digit number = Square of that number
$$D(a) = a^2$$
  Duplex of $2 = 2^2 = 4$
  Duplex of $6 = 6^2 = 36$
- Duplex of 2-digit number = $2 \times$ (product of digits)
$$D(ab) = 2ab$$
  Duplex of $24 = 2 \times (2 \times 4) = 16$
  Duplex of $76 = 2 \times (7 \times 6) = 84$
- Duplex of 3-digit number = $2 \times$ (1st digit $\times$ 3rd digit) + (square of middle digit)
$$D(abc) = 2ac + b^2$$
  Duplex of $126 = 2 \times (1 \times 6) + 2^2 = 16$
  Duplex of $478 = 2 \times (4 \times 8) + 7^2 = 113$

Example 1: Find the square of 49.

Solution: The groups for 49 are

$$\underbrace{D(4)}_{} \qquad \underbrace{D(49)}_{} \qquad \underbrace{D(9)}_{}$$

= 4^2 | $2 \times 4 \times 9$ | 9^2

= 16 | 72 | 81

= 16 | 80 | 1

= 2401

Example 2: $41^2 + 35^2$

Solution:

Step 1: D4 + D3 = 16 + 9 = 25

Step 2: D41 + D35 = $2 \times 4 \times 1 + 2 \times 3 \times 5 = 38$

Step 3: D1 + D5 = 1 + 25 = 26

Arrange the results obtained with the help of separators.

25 | 38 | 26

= 28 | 10 | 6

= 2906

Example 3: $116^2 + 231^2$

Solution:

Step 1: D1 + D2 = 1 + 4 = 5

Step 2: D11 + D23 = $2 \times 1 \times 1 + 2 \times 2 \times 3 = 14$

Step 3: D116 + D231 = $2 \times 1 \times 6 + 1^2 + 2 \times 2 \times 1 + 3^2 = 26$

Step 4: D16 + D31 = $2 \times 1 \times 6 + 2 \times 3 \times 1 = 18$

Step 5: D6 + D1 = 37

Arrange the results obtained with the help of separators.

5 | 14 | 26| 18| 37
= 5 + 1 | 4 + 2 | 6 + 1 | 8 + 3 | 7
= 6 | 6 | 7 |11 | 7
= 6 | 6 | 8 | 1 | 7
= 66817

Once you are familiar with addition, subtraction, multiplication and other methods of Vedic Mathematics, you can do multiple operations at a time. Even tough operations like square root and cube root can be done in seconds using Vedic Mathematics.

12

Harder Factor

Introduction

Generally, we deal with factors of a polynomial with one variable, such as factorizing quadratic or cubic polynomials, or factors of polynomials with two variables. The methods we have learnt so far are breaking the polynomials into smaller parts, using factor theorem, and mid-term factorization. Let's consider a case where a second-degree polynomial has more than two variables. Arranging such polynomials into smaller ones is not an easy task, and factorizing them is a Herculean task. Here comes the Vedic sutra, **Lopansthapanabhyam**, which reduces the big polynomials into smaller ones and factorization becomes easy.

Lopansthapanabhyam means 'by elimination and retention'. Here we eliminate different variables one by one while retaining other variables, so as to factorize them easily. This sutra is highly applicable when solving the co-ordinate geometry problems of a straight line, hyperbola, asymptotes etc.

Example 1: Factorize $x^2 + xy - 2y^2 + 2xz - 5yz - 3z^2$

Solution: Here you can see that the given equation is a three-variable equation in degree 2 (the highest power of the variable is 2). We can't even apply the formula:

$(a + b + c)^2 = a^2 + b^2 + c^2 + 2ab + 2bc + 2ca$

Here comes the Vedic sutra for solving the equation easily. The traditional method will only confuse you, as we need to add some variable to get the complete factor and reduce the whole equation into three factors and then into two. Let's see how to work using the Vedic sutra.

This higher order polynomial involves three variables – x, y and z. Let's start by eliminating x. Putting x = 0, we have

$$- 2y^2 - 5yz - 3z^2$$

Factorizing the reduced polynomial, we have

$$- 2y^2 - 5yz - 3z^2 = - (y + z)(2y + 3z) \quad ...(1)$$

Now putting y = 0, we have

$x^2 + 2xz - 3z^2$ and this can be further reduced to $(x + 3z)$ $(x - z)$ ...(2)

Let's now eliminate z and put z = 0

$$x^2 + xy - 2y^2 = x^2 + 2xy - xy - 2y^2$$
$$= (x + 2y)(x - y) \quad\quad ...(3)$$

On observing the three equations we may conclude the cyclic nature of the factor. We have + 2y and + 3z and + x in each of the two equations, hence (x + 2y + 3z) is one of the factors, and the other factor, in a similar manner, can be arranged as (x – y – z).

Therefore,

$$x^2 + xy - 2y^2 + 2xz - 5yz - 3z^2 = (x + 2y + 3z)(x - y - z)$$

Example 2: Factorize $3x^2 + 10y^2 + 3z^2 + 17xy + 11yz + 10xz$

Solution: Start eliminating one variable at a time as discussed in the previous example.

Put $x = 0$, and we have

$$10y^2 + 11yz + 3z^2 = 10y^2 + 5yz + 6yz + 3z^2$$
$$= (2y + z)(5y + 3z)$$

Put $y = 0$

$$3x^2 + 10xz + 3z^2 = (x + 3z)(3x + z)$$

Put $z = 0$

$$3x^2 + 17xy + 10y^2 = (x + 5y)(3x + 2y)$$

Observing the cyclic nature of factors, we can directly write:

$$3x^2 + 10y^2 + 3z^2 + 17xy + 11yz + 10xz = (x + 5y + 3z)(3x + 2y + z)$$

Example 3: Factorize $2x^2 - 3y^2 - 2z^2 + 5xy - 5yz + 3xz$

Solution: First put $x = 0$ and eliminate x.

$$- 3y^2 - 5yz - 2z^2$$
$$= - (3y^2 + 5yz + 2z^2)$$
$$= - (3y^2 + 3yz + 2yz + 2z^2)$$
$$= - (3y + 2z)(y + z) \qquad \qquad ...(1)$$

Put $y = 0$

$$2x^2 + 3xz - 2z^2 = (x + 2z)(2x - z) \qquad ...(2)$$

Put $z = 0$

$$2x^2 + 5xy - 3y^2 = (x + 3y)(2x - y) \qquad ...(3)$$

Combining all three and checking with the common factors, we can write

$$2x^2 - 3y^2 - 2z^2 + 5xy - 5yz + 3xz = (x + 3y + 2z)(2x - y - z)$$

Let's explore it with one more example.

Example 4: Factorize $2m^2 + 2n^2 - 5mn - 7m - n - 15$

Solution: Putting m = 0, we have

$2n^2 - n - 15 = (n - 3)(2n + 5)$

Put n = 0, we have

$2m^2 - 7m - 15 = (m - 5)(2m + 3)$

Here, 3 and 5 are common factors but with opposite signs. Let's rearrange the terms to get the same sign.

$$2n^2 - n - 15 = (n - 3)(2n + 5)$$
$$= (3 - n)(-2n - 5) \qquad ...(1)$$

Multiplying by $1 = -1 \times -1$

[Here, both factorable expressions are multiplied by -1.
$(-1) \times (3 - n) \times (-1) \times (2n + 5) = (3 - n)(-2n - 5)$]

Moreover, we have

$2m^2 - 7m - 15 = (m - 5)(2m + 3) \qquad ...(2)$

Now, in equations 1 and 2 we can see that + 3 and − 5 have common terms, so the combined factor of the given polynomial can be written as:

$$2m^2 + 2n^2 - 5mn - 7m - n - 15 = (m - 2n - 5)(2m - n + 3)$$

In the above example, I eliminated only two variables and got the answer. Look at some other examples and try to explore the fact that harder polynomials can be factorized easily even by eliminating only two variables.

13

Determinant

Introduction

If $A = [a_{ij}]$ is a square matrix of order n, then we can associate a number called the determinant of the square matrix A, where a_{ij} = (i, j)th element of A.

$A = \begin{bmatrix} 0 & 3 \\ 5 & 4 \end{bmatrix}$ is a square matrix of order 2, as it has 2 rows and 2 columns. A matrix is therefore the arrangement of numbers in such a way that we have rows and columns written in square or rectangular form. If a matrix has more rows than columns, then we call it a rectangular matrix.

In simple words, it is an arrangement of elements in rows and columns, which are in square or rectangular form.

A determinant of a 2 × 2 order has 4 elements. Similarly, a determinant of a 3 × 3 order has 9 elements and a determinant of a 4 × 4 order has 16 elements.

Properties of a determinant

- If we interchange any two rows or columns in a determinant then the sign of a determinant changes.

- If any two rows or columns are identical or proportional, then the value of the determinant is zero.
- If all the elements of a row or a column are zeros, then the value of the determinant is zero.
- If we multiply each element of a row or a column of a determinant by the constant term k, then the value of the determinant is multiplied by k.
- If each element of one row or column of a determinant is a sum of 2 terms, then the determinant can be expressed as a sum of 2 terms.

Let's first see how a determinant is solved in the traditional method.

Example 1: $\begin{vmatrix} 7 & 2 \\ 5 & 3 \end{vmatrix}$

Solution: It is a 2 × 2 determinant which can be easily solved using the cross multiplication method.

$$\begin{vmatrix} 7 & 2 \\ 5 & 3 \end{vmatrix} = 7 \times 3 - 5 \times 2 = 21 - 10 = 11$$

Determinant of order 3 × 3:

Determinant of a matrix of order 3 can be solved by expanding along a row or column. There are six ways to solve a determinant, three along rows and three along columns.

Expansion along first row:

If A is a matrix such that its determinant is

$$|A| = \begin{vmatrix} a_{11} & a_{12} & a_{13} \\ a_{21} & a_{22} & a_{23} \\ a_{31} & a_{32} & a_{33} \end{vmatrix}$$

multiply first element of row 1, i.e. R_1 with the second order determinant obtained by deleting the elements of the first row (R_1) and the first column (C_1).

$$a_{11} \begin{vmatrix} a_{22} & a_{23} \\ a_{32} & a_{33} \end{vmatrix}$$

Multiply second element of row 1 by negative times the second order determinant obtained by deleting elements of the first row (R_1) and the second column (C_2).

$$a_{12} \begin{vmatrix} a_{21} & a_{23} \\ a_{31} & a_{33} \end{vmatrix}$$

Multiply third element of row 1 by the second order determinant obtained by deleting elements of the first row (R_1) and the third column (C_3).

$$a_{13} \begin{vmatrix} a_{21} & a_{22} \\ a_{31} & a_{32} \end{vmatrix}$$

Combining the three steps discussed above, we can solve a 3 by 3 determinant.

$$|A| = a_{11} \begin{vmatrix} a_{22} & a_{23} \\ a_{32} & a_{33} \end{vmatrix} - a_{12} \begin{vmatrix} a_{21} & a_{23} \\ a_{31} & a_{33} \end{vmatrix} + a_{13} \begin{vmatrix} a_{21} & a_{22} \\ a_{31} & a_{32} \end{vmatrix}$$

$$a_{11}(a_{22}a_{33} - a_{32}a_{23}) - a_{12}(a_{21}a_{33} - a_{31}a_{23}) + a_{13}(a_{21}a_{32} - a_{31}a_{22})$$

Example 2: Solve $\begin{vmatrix} 2 & 5 & -3 \\ 0 & 1 & 7 \\ 1 & 4 & 2 \end{vmatrix}$

Solution:

$$\begin{vmatrix} 2 & 5 & -3 \\ 0 & 1 & 7 \\ 1 & 4 & 2 \end{vmatrix}$$

$$= 2 \begin{vmatrix} 1 & 7 \\ 4 & 2 \end{vmatrix} - 5 \begin{vmatrix} 0 & 7 \\ 1 & 2 \end{vmatrix} + (-3) \begin{vmatrix} 0 & 1 \\ 1 & 4 \end{vmatrix}$$

$$= 2 (2 - 28) - 5 (0 - 7) - 3 (0 - 1)$$

$$= 2 \times -26 + 35 + 3$$

$$= -52 + 38$$

$$= -14$$

Now let's move to the Vedic way of solving the determinant. Determinant of order 2 is easy to solve, so let's concentrate on solving a 3 × 3 determinant.

Let's say we have the following determinant of order 3 × 3.

$$\begin{vmatrix} a_1 & b_1 & c_1 \\ a_2 & b_2 & c_2 \\ a_3 & b_3 & c_3 \end{vmatrix}$$

First, separate the first or third row by a line as shown here.

$$\begin{array}{|ccc|} a_1 & b_1 & c_1 \\ \hline a_2 & b_2 & c_2 \\ a_3 & b_3 & c_3 \end{array} \qquad \text{or} \qquad \begin{array}{|ccc|} a_1 & b_1 & c_1 \\ a_2 & b_2 & c_2 \\ \hline a_3 & b_3 & c_3 \end{array}$$

From the remaining two rows make three determinants of 2 × 2 in the order of column 12, 13 and 23.

$$\begin{array}{|ccc|} a_1 & b_1 & c_1 \\ \hline a_2 & b_2 & c_2 \\ a_3 & b_3 & c_3 \end{array}$$

$$a_2 b_3 - a_3 b_2 \qquad a_2 c_3 - a_3 c_2 \qquad b_2 c_3 - b_3 c_2$$

Now place the value obtained above on the top of a 3 × 3 cross multiplication method of **Urdhva Tiryag,** and the first row element at the bottom of the cross, as shown here.

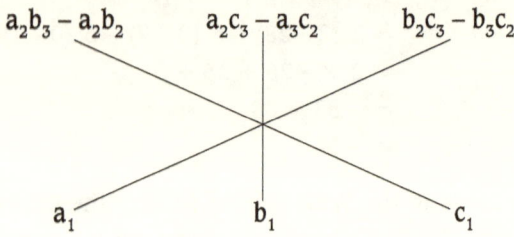

$a_2b_3 - a_2b_2$ $a_2c_3 - a_3c_2$ $b_2c_3 - b_3c_2$

a_1 b_1 c_1

On solving it you will have the solution of the determinant.

Hence, $|A| = a_1 (b_2c_3 - b_3c_2) - b_1 (a_2c_3 - a_3c_2) + c_1 (a_2b_3 - a_3b_2)$

Let's see some examples.

Example 3: Find the value of $\begin{vmatrix} 1 & 3 & 5 \\ 6 & 1 & 7 \\ 1 & 2 & 4 \end{vmatrix}$

Solution: First draw a line to separate the first row from the others and solve the 2 by 2 columnwise determinant by the column 12, 13, 23, and write down the result below the third row.

$$\begin{array}{|ccc|} \hline 1 & 3 & 5 \\ \hline 6 & 1 & 7 \\ 11 & 17 & -10 \\ \hline \end{array}$$

Now place the value in a cross at the top as discussed above and write the first row below as shown, and solve.

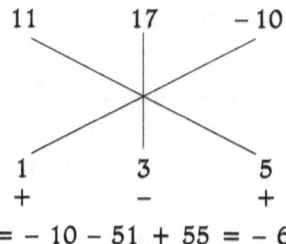

$$= -10 - 51 + 55 = -6$$

Example 4: Solve the given determinant.

$$\begin{vmatrix} 5 & 2 & 11 \\ 3 & 6 & 1 \\ 4 & 5 & 7 \end{vmatrix}$$

Solution: First draw a line to separate the first row from the others and solve the 2 by 2 columnwise determinant by the column 12, 13, 23, and write down the result below the third row.

$$\begin{array}{|ccc|}
\hline
5 & 2 & 11 \\
\hline
3 & 6 & 1 \\
4 & 5 & 7 \\
-9 & 17 & 37 \\
\end{array}$$

Now place the value in a cross at the top as discussed above and write the first row below, as shown, and solve.

$$
\begin{array}{ccc}
-9 & 17 & 37 \\
 & & \\
5 & 2 & 11 \\
+ & - & + \\
\end{array}
$$

$$= -99 + 34 + 185$$
$$= 120$$

Solving a determinant of order 4 by 4:

It is a big challenge to solve a 4 by 4 determinant by the traditional method as we need to break it into four determinants of order 3 by 3, followed by 12 determinants of order 2 by 2 to solve, but the Vedic Method—Urdhva Tiryag—will help solve it without breaking it into so many determinants. Let's see how to proceed with a determinant of order 4 by 4.

Step 1: Draw a line bifurcating the determinant into 2 parts such that there are 2 rows above and below the drawn line.

Step 2: Make 6 determinants above and below the bifurcated line. The order of 2 x 2 determinants taken columnwise will be 12, 13, 14, 23, 24 and 34.

Step 3: Place the obtained values at their respective places in order, above and below. Once you are ready with the values, place it on the cross. The value at the top will be the value of the determinant obtained at the top of the dotted line and the value at the bottom of the cross will be the value of the determinant obtained at the bottom of the dotted line.

Example 1: Solve:

$$\begin{vmatrix} 2 & 1 & 3 & 4 \\ 3 & 0 & -2 & -1 \\ 1 & 4 & 3 & 7 \\ 0 & 2 & 5 & 1 \end{vmatrix}$$

Solution: Draw a line so that the whole determinant is divided into two halves. Solve each of the 2×2 columnwise determinants in the order of 12, 13, 14, 23, 24 and 34. Write the value of each determinant's solution in its respective place, as shown here.

$$-3 \ -13 \ -14 \ -2 \ -1 \ 5$$

$$\begin{vmatrix} 2 & 1 & 3 & 4 \\ 3 & 0 & -2 & -1 \\ 1 & 4 & 3 & 7 \\ 0 & 2 & 5 & 1 \end{vmatrix}$$

$$2 \ 5 \ 1 \ 14 \ -10 \ -32$$
$$+ \ - \ + \ + \ - \ +$$

Now draw a cross diagram and place these values with the corrected sign of the bottom determinant value.

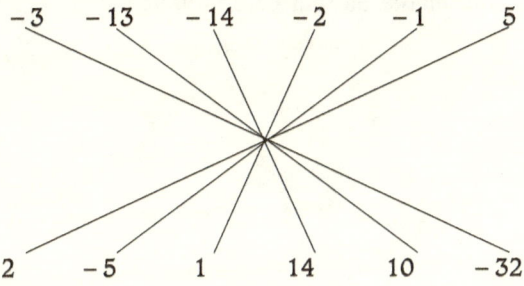

Now solve it and get the final result.
$$96 - 130 - 196 - 2 + 5 + 10 = -217$$

Example 2: Solve the given determinant.

$$\begin{vmatrix} 2 & 1 & 4 & 3 \\ 3 & -2 & -2 & 4 \\ -1 & -3 & 1 & -4 \\ 2 & 1 & 3 & 2 \end{vmatrix}$$

Solution: Draw a line so that the whole determinant is divided into two halves. Solve each of the 2 × 2 columnwise determinants in the order of 12, 13, 14, 23, 24 and 34. Write the value of each determinant solution at its respective place as shown below.

$$
\begin{array}{cccccc}
-7 & -16 & -1 & 6 & 10 & 22 \\
\end{array}
$$

$$
\begin{vmatrix}
2 & 1 & 4 & 3 \\
3 & -2 & -2 & 4 \\
\end{vmatrix}
$$

$$
\begin{vmatrix}
-1 & -3 & 1 & -4 \\
2 & 1 & 3 & 2 \\
\end{vmatrix}
$$

$$
\begin{array}{cccccc}
5 & -5 & 6 & -10 & -2 & 14 \\
+ & - & + & + & - & + \\
\end{array}
$$

Now draw a cross diagram and place these values with the corrected sign of the bottom determinant value.

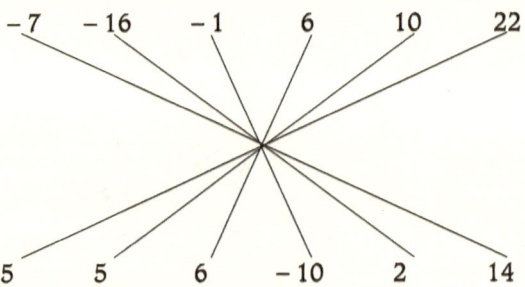

Hence the value of the determinant is

= 110 + 50 + 36 + 10 – 32 – 98

= 76

Hope you have enjoyed the Urdhva Tiryag method of solving determinants. Keep exploring the new technique and learn how to solve even the toughest of problems quickly.

14

Coordinate Geometry

Introduction

Coordinate geometry is a branch of geometry where the position of each point on a plane is defined with the help of an ordered pair of numbers known as coordinates. The x-point is called the abscissa and y-point is called the ordinate of the given position.

Rene Descartes was the pioneer and the father of coordinate geometry. In a plane, if we draw a horizontal line called the x-axis and a vertical line called the y-axis then they intersect at a point called the origin. These two lines divide the whole plane into four parts called quadrants.

1st quadrant	$(+, +)$
2nd quadrant	$(-, +)$
3rd quadrant	$(-, -)$
4th quadrant	$(+, -)$

The locations of the points in the respective quadrants decide the positions of the points and their respective abscissa or ordinates.

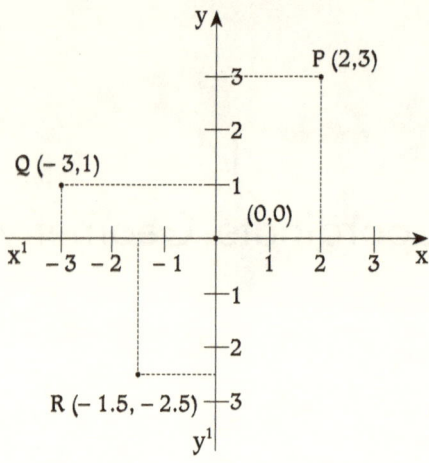

Here we shall deal with a few Vedic methods to solve the problems of coordinate geometry. It is to be remembered that Vedic Mathematics is not rocket science, so you need to remember all the conditions related to geometrical shapes, and their properties too. Suppose you have to prove a given triangle is a right-angled triangle. Vedic Mathematics will help you to calculate the length of all the three sides quickly, but you need to be aware of Baudhayana or the Pythagoras Theorem to prove it.

Now let's first start with the most common formula—Distance Formula, used to find the distance between two points.

Distance formula

If A (x_1, y_1) and B (x_2, y_2) are two points on a co-ordinate plane, then distance between A and B is defined as

$$AB = \sqrt{(x_2 - x_1)^2 + (y_2 - y_1)^2}$$

This can be better understood with the facts that if A (a, b) and B (c, d) are two points on a Cartesian plane, then their distance is

$$\sqrt{a^2 + b^2 + c^2 + d^2 - 2(ab + cd)}$$

This simply means that if we sum up the squares of each point and subtract twice the product of the coordinates from the sum of the squares and take its square root, then we have the distance between two points.

Example 1: Find the distance between (1, 3) and (2, 0).

Solution: Here a = 1, b = 3, c = 2 and d = 0
   Hence distance =

$$\sqrt{a^2 + b^2 + c^2 + d^2 - 2(ac + bd)}$$
$$= \sqrt{(-1)^2 + 3^2 + (-2)^2 + 0^2 - 2(-1 \times -2 + 3 \times 0)} = \sqrt{10} \text{ unit}$$

Example 2: Find the distance between (4, 3) and (2, 5).

Solution: Here a = 4, b = 3, c = 2 and d = 5
   Hence distance =

$$\sqrt{a^2 + b^2 + c^2 + d^2 - 2(ac + bd)}$$
$$= \sqrt{(4)^2 + 3^2 + (-2)^2 + 5^2 - 2(4 \times -2 + 3 \times 5)} = \sqrt{40} = 2\sqrt{10} \text{ unit}$$

Example 3: Find the distance between (x, y) and (−x, −y).

Solution: Here a = x, b = y, c = −x, d = −y
   Hence distance =

$$\sqrt{a^2 + b^2 + c^2 + d^2 - 2(ac + bd)}$$
$$= \sqrt{x^2 + y^2 + (-x)^2 + (-y)^2 - 2(x \times -x + -y \times -x)}$$
$$= \sqrt{4x^2 + 4y^2} \text{ units}$$

Example 4: Find the distance of a point P (−2, 5) from the origin.

Solution: Here a = 0, b = 0, c = 2 and d = 5

Hence distance =

$$\sqrt{a^2 + b^2 + c^2 + d^2 - 2(ac + bd)}$$

$$= \sqrt{(0)^2 + 0^2 + (-2)^2 + 5^2 - 2(0 \times -2 + 0 \times 5)} = \sqrt{41} = \text{unit}$$

Section formula

The section formula tells us the coordinates of the point which divides the line segment into some ratio. The division may be internal or external.

Internal Division

A(x_1, y_1) m P(x, y) n B(x_2, y_2)

Let P (x, y) divide the line segment AB in m:n ratio. Then the coordinates x and y can be obtained using the section formula. Here P divides the line segment internally.

This is nothing but the crosswise multiplication commonly used in Vedic Mathematics.

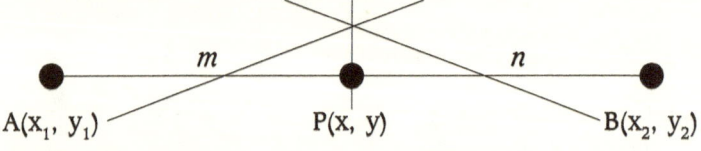

m P(x, y) n

A(x_1, y_1)   P(x, y)   B(x_2, y_2)

Minute observation tells us that in order to find the value of the x-coordinate, simply write the cross product of the ratio with the x-coordinate and divide it with the sum of the ratio.

$$x = \frac{mx_2 + nx_1}{m + n} \quad \text{and} \quad y = \frac{my_2 + ny_1}{m + n}$$

If m and n are equal, then point P divides the line segment equally and the coordinate of midpoint P is given as $\left(\dfrac{x_1 + x_2}{2}, \dfrac{y_1 + y_2}{2}\right)$.

Example 1: Find the coordinates of the point that divides the line segment joining the points (2, 5) and (1, 9) in the ratio of 2:3.

Solution:

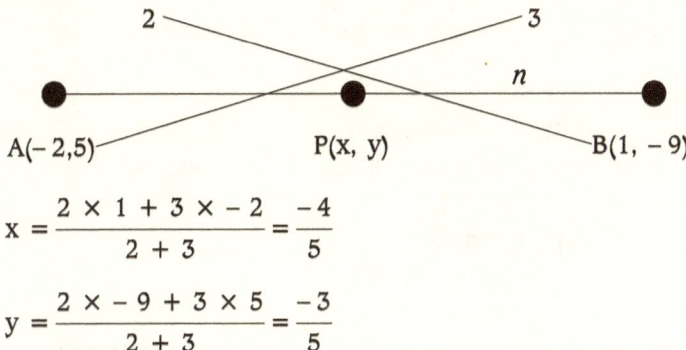

$$x = \frac{2 \times 1 + 3 \times -2}{2 + 3} = \frac{-4}{5}$$

$$y = \frac{2 \times -9 + 3 \times 5}{2 + 3} = \frac{-3}{5}$$

Example 2: In what ratio does the y-axis divide the line of (7, 3) and (5, 12)?

Solution: Let the ratio be k:1.

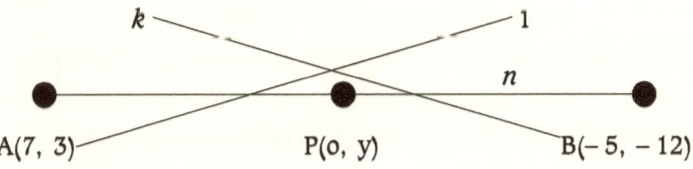

On y-axis the x-coordinate is 0.

$$0 = \frac{-5k + 7}{k + 1}$$

So, 5k = 7

Hence, k = 7/5

Drawing a graph of a linear equation

A linear equation in two variables can be easily plotted on a graph by elimination and retention method. In simple language, Vilokanam sutra is helpful to judge the point where the line will intersect the axes.

Example 1: Draw the graph of 2x + 3y = 12

Solution: Put x = 0 ⇒ y = 4
        Put y = 0 ⇒ x = 6

On the x-axis, mark a circle at point x = 6, and on the y-axis mark a point at y = 4.

    Join these two circles.

    Now this is the graph of 2x + 3y = 12.

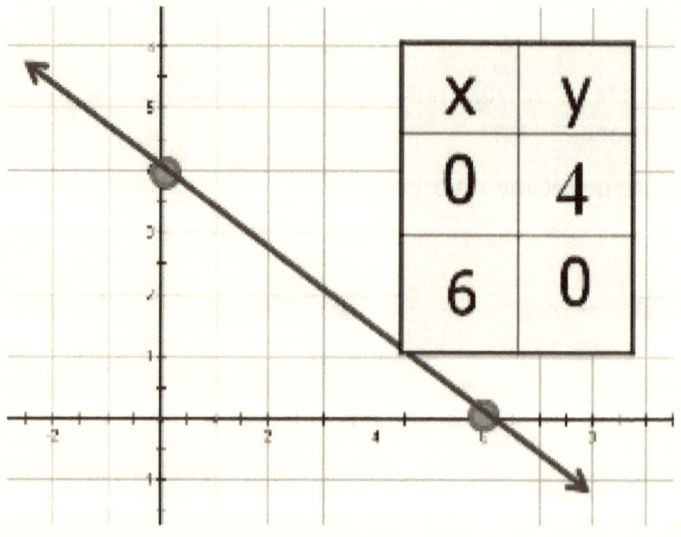

x	y
0	4
6	0

The graph can easily be constructed by applying the intercept formula. $x/a + y/b = 1$

First divide the graph equation by 12 to make the RHS = 1.

$2/12x + 3/12y = 12/12 = 1$

$$\Rightarrow x/6 + y/4 = 1$$

The next step is simple. Simply take the intercepts 6 and 4 on x- and y-axis respectively.

Example 2: Draw the graph of $x + 2y = 6$

Solution: Put $x = 0 \Rightarrow y = 3$

Put $y = 0 \Rightarrow x = 6$

Mark these two points on the coordinate axis and draw the graph.

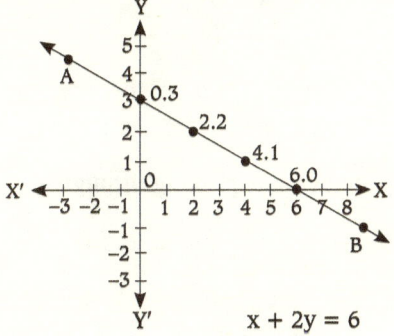

$x + 2y = 6$

Equation of line passing through two points

Basically, in the intermediate syllabus we have to find the equation of a line passing through one point or two, and we apply the relevant formula.

Finding out the equation of a line passing through one point (x_1, y_1) with a slope or a gradient m is defined as:

$$\frac{y - y_1}{x - x_1} = m$$

Example 1: Find the equation of the line passing through (0, 5) with slope 1/2.

Solution: Equation of line

$$\frac{y - y_1}{x - x_1} = m$$

Hence, equation of line passing through (0, 5) with slope 1/2 is

$$\frac{y - 5}{x - 0} = \frac{1}{2}$$
$$\Rightarrow x - 2y = -10$$

Example 2: Find the equation of the line passing through (0, 0) that makes an angle of 45° with the axes.

Solution: Equation of a line passing through (0, 0) and making an angle $\theta = 45$ is $\frac{y - y_1}{x - x_1} = m = \tan \theta$

$$\Rightarrow \frac{y - 0}{x - 0} = \tan 45 = 1$$
$$\Rightarrow y - x$$

When it comes to finding the equation of a line passing through two points, we have a general formula that we use:

$$\frac{y - y_1}{x - x_1} = \frac{y_2 - y_1}{x_2 - x_1}$$

Example 3: Find the equation of a line passing through (3, 4) and (8, 10).

Solution: Here, $x_1 = 3$, $y_1 = 4$, $x_2 = 8$ and $y_2 = 10$.

Equation of line $= \dfrac{y - 4}{x - 3} = \dfrac{10 - 4}{8 - 3}$

$\Rightarrow 5y - 20 = 6x - 18$

$\Rightarrow 5y - 6x - 2 = 0$

This method is tedious as the calculation is lengthy. Let's solve it using the Vedic method. The Vertical and Crosswise and Transpose and Apply methods will be applicable here. Let's see the working.

The equation is:

$ax - by = c$

$\Rightarrow$ (Difference of y-coordinate)x − (difference of x- coordinate)y + product of means − product of extremes

$\Rightarrow (4 - 10)x - (3 - 8)y + 3 \times 10 - 4 \times 8 = 0$

$\Rightarrow -6x + 5y - 2 = 0$

It can be easily done by writing things row-wise one below the other. Let's see how this works.

$$\begin{array}{ccc} x_1 \Big\downarrow & y_1 \Big\downarrow & c = \begin{vmatrix} x_1 & y_1 \\ x_2 & y_2 \end{vmatrix} \\ x_2 & y_2 & \end{array}$$

Equation: $(x_1 - x_2)y = (y_1 - y_2)x + (x_1 y_2 - x_2 y_1)$

Example 4: Find the equation of the line passing through (4, 7) and (6, 3).

Solution:

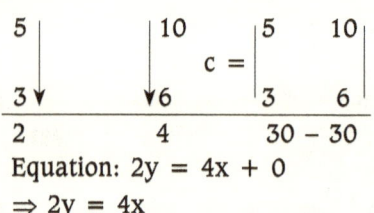

$$- 3y = 3x - 30$$

Example 5: Find the equation of the line passing through (5, 10) and (3, 6).

Solution:

$$\begin{array}{ccc} 5 & 10 & \qquad c = \begin{vmatrix} 5 & 10 \\ 3 & 6 \end{vmatrix} \\ 3 & 6 \\ \hline 2 & 4 & 30 - 30 \end{array}$$

Equation: $2y = 4x + 0$

$\Rightarrow 2y = 4x$

Equation of line parallel and perpendicular to a given line

Example 1: Find the equation of a line parallel to $3x + 5y = 17$ passing through (2, 1).

Solution: Equation of a line passing through (2, 1) is
$3 \times 2 + 5 \times 1 = 11$

Hence, equation of a line parallel to $3x + 5y = 17$ is
$3x + 5y = 11$

Example 2: Find the equation of a line passing through (– 5, 11) and parallel to $2x + y = 7$

Solution: Equation of a line passing through (– 5, 11) is

$2 \times -5 + 11 = 1$

Hence, equation of a line parallel to $2x + y = 7$ is $2x + y = 1$

Example 3: Find the equation of a line passing through (2, 5) and parallel to $3x + 5y = 13$.

Solution: We know that two lines are perpendicular to each other if the product of their slope is − 1. Hence, to find the equation of a line perpendicular to a given line, first swap the coefficients and change the sign between their variables.

Therefore, the equation of the line is:

$5x − 3y = 5 \times 2 − 3 \times 5.$

$\Rightarrow 5x − 3y = − 5$

Triples and its use in coordinate geometry

Let me provide a brief account of triples. Triples, better known as the Pythagorean triple, is the relation between the three sides of a right-angled triangle.

$\text{Hypotenuse}^2 = (\text{Perpendicular})^2 + (\text{Base})^2$

Triples have been in use since long before Pythagoras was born. Around 800 BC, saints used to construct yagna kunds to worship deities, and these kunds used to follow the so-called Baudhayana Theorem—better known as the **Pythagoras Theorem**. The Pythagoras Theorem establishes the relation between base, perpendicular and hypotenuse. In much of the Sulva sutra, there are references to the relation between the perpendicular, base and hypotenuse.

Let's look at the following chart that tells us about the different triples being used during the Vedic era.

Mr T.K. Puttaswamy, in his book, *Mathematical Achievements of Pre-modern Indian Mathematicians,* clearly mentions that the author of Sulva sutra had the knowledge of triples, and while performing yajna and making an altar thereof, the size of the Yagna Kunda they were taking followed the Pythagorean triples. The following right triangles have been mentioned in the Sulva sutra.

Perpendicular	Base	Hypotenuse	Author of Sulva sutra
3	4	5	Apasthamba / Baudhayana
5	12	13	Apasthamba / Baudhayana
7	24	25	Apasthamba / Baudhayana
12	35	37	Apasthamba / Baudhayana
15	36	39	Apasthamba / Baudhayana
2½	6	6½	Manava
7½	10	12½	Manava
40	96	104	Manava
72	96	120	Manava

The so-called triple given here is the basic triple and it can be constructed for different angles.

Triple for 45° –	1,	1	√2
Triple for 30° –	√3,	1	2
Triple for 90° –	0,	1	1

Triples are easy to understand. Once you memorize these values, you can find the angle between two lines.

Angle between two lines

In coordinate geometry, the angle between two lines can be measured by subtracting the triples of the given lines.

Consider the following two trigonometry ratios for two different angles A and B. If B, P, H and b, p, h are the triples of two angles A and B respectively, then the triples for the difference of angles is given by:

A	B	P	H
B	b	p	h
A − B	Bb + Pb	Pb − Bp	Hh

Example 1: Find the angle between two lines $3x - y + 2 = 0$ and $3y + x = 7$.

Solution:

Line 1	1	3	$\sqrt{10}$
Line 2	3	− 1	$\sqrt{10}$
Difference	3 − 3	3 × 3 − 1 × −1	10
	0	10	10

Since the first element of a triple is zero, the two lines are perpendicular to each other.

Example 2: Find the angle between two lines $y - 2x = 5$ and $3y = x - 2$.

Solution:

Line 1	3	1	$\sqrt{10}$
Line 2	1	2	$\sqrt{5}$
Triples	3 + 2	1 − 6	$\sqrt{50}$
	5	− 5	

Since the sign (+, −) can be neglected, the angle between the two lines = $|5/-5| = 1$

$$\tan \theta = 1$$
$$\Rightarrow \theta = 45°$$

Length of perpendicular to a given line from a given point

You must have remembered the formula to find the distance of a given line from a point outside the line.

For a given line, $Ax + By + C = 0$. The perpendicular distance from a point (m, n) is given by:

$$d = \frac{|Am + Bn + C|}{\sqrt{A^2 + B^2}}$$

In Vedic Mathematics, you can find the distance with the help of the triples of the given line and point. First, subtract the triples of the line and point and then divide the combined triples by the hypotenuse of the first triple.

Example 1: Find the distance of the line $2y = x$ from the point $(3, 4)$.

Solution: First write the triples of the given line and point and subtract them to get new triples.

Line 1	2	1	$\sqrt{5}$
Point	3	4	–
Subtract	6 + 4	3 – 8	–
	10	– 5	

Perpendicular distance = Combined triple of Base / Hypotenuse of first line

$$= \frac{5}{\sqrt{5}} = \sqrt{5} \text{ unit}$$

Example 2: Find the perpendicular distance of a given line $5x + 12y = 13$ from the point $(2, 3)$.

Solution: First you need to check whether the given line passes through the origin or not. If the given line whose distance from a given point is to be found doesn't pass through the origin then the concept of shifting the origin will be used to determine the value.

Let's put $x = 1$ in $5x + 12y = 13$

$$\Rightarrow 5 + 12y = 13$$
$$\Rightarrow y = 8/12$$

Shifting the origin will give you a new coordinate.

New coordinate $(2 - 1, 3 - 8/12) = (1, 28/12)$

We have $5x + 12y = 13$

$$\Rightarrow 12y = -5x + 13$$

Let's find the distance:

Line	12	– 5	13
Point	1	28/12	–
Subtract	12 – 140/12	– 5 – 28	
	4/12		– 33

Perpendicular distance = Combined triple of base / Hypotenuse of first line

$$= \frac{|-33|}{13} = 33/13 \text{ unit}$$

As seen in the above examples, Vedic Mathematics may prove to be a boon not only for students but also for researchers. We must endeavour to save the ancient wisdom of the nation by finding the hidden jewels in the Vedic sutras.

15

Differentiation

Introduction

Calculus is one of the most important branches of mathematics. It was independently discovered by Isaac Newton and Leibniz but a brief concept of calculus was discovered much earlier by Bhaskaracharya. The Kerala School of Mathematics did a remarkable job in the expansion of the Taylor, sine and cosine series, but it was not seen the way we see calculus in the present time.

The Taylor series, sine series and cosine series were discovered in India much earlier by Madhava, the founder of the Kerala School of Mathematics.

The Taylor series of a real or complex function f(x), that is infinitely differentiable at a real or complex number a, is a power series and can be written as:

$$f(a) + \frac{f'(a)}{1!}(x - a) + \frac{f''(a)}{2!}(x - a)^2 + \frac{f'''(a)}{3!}(x - a)^3 + \dots$$

The sine and cosine series can also be written as:

$$\cos x = 1 - \frac{x^2}{2!} + \frac{x^4}{4!} -$$

$$\sin x = x - \frac{x^3}{3!} + \frac{x^5}{5!} -$$

It has significant applications in science and engineering. Calculus is basically the branch of mathematics that deals with continuous change. It has two parts—Differentiation and Integration. Here we shall deal with a simple differentiation technique, that will be done using Vedic Mathematics.

$$\frac{dy}{dx} = \frac{f(x + dx) - f(x)}{dx}$$

As we know, the above formula will help us in differentiation. An important aspect of differentiation comes in the chain rule method. Here we shall deal with chain rule and double differentiation of a given function.

Differentiation of power form

The power forms such as x^{10}, x^{100}, x^{1024}... etc. can be obtained by applying the **Eknyunen Purven** sutra. In the first part of the book on Vedic Mathematics, *The Essentials of Vedic Mathematics*, we have put this sutra to good use. The modern formula is similar to the Eknyunen Purven sutra.

We know that

$$\frac{d(x^n)}{dx} = nx^{n-1}$$

It simply says that in order to differentiate any variable in power, simply multiply the power with the variable, with the latter's power now lowered by 1.

$$\frac{d(x^5)}{dx} = 5x^4$$

If we have $y = x^5$ as a function then dy/dx is called the first differential, denoted by y_1 or y'. This can be further differentiated in a similar way. y'' or y_2 is the second differential and is denoted by d^2y/dx^2, y''' or y_3 is the third differential, and so on.

Hence for $y = x^4$

$y' = 4x^3$

$y'' = 4 \times 3x^2 = 12x^2$

$y''' = 24x^1$

$y'''' = 24x^0$

$y''''' = 0$

Thus the differentiation of the constant term is zero.

Before we proceed with the chain rule of the given function, we need to learn a few formulas related to differentiation.

$\dfrac{d(\sin x)}{dx} = \cos x$	$\dfrac{d(\cos x)}{dx} = -\sin x$
$\dfrac{d(\tan x)}{dx} = \sec^2 x$	$\dfrac{d(\cot x)}{dx} = -\operatorname{cosec}^2 x$
$\dfrac{d(\sec x)}{dx} = \sec x.\tan x$	$\dfrac{d(\operatorname{cosec} x)}{dx} = -\operatorname{cosec} x.\cot x$
$\dfrac{d(\log x)}{dx} = 1/x$	$\dfrac{d(\sqrt{x})}{dx} = 1/2\sqrt{x}$

Chain rule

Another important aspect of differentiation is the chain rule. The chain rule is a loop of differentiation functions until we reach a function whose differentiation can be done with respect to x, and the function is independent of any other function except x. Consider the following examples:

a) $f(x) = \sqrt{x}$ b) $g(x) = \log x$ c) $h(x) = e^x$

All these functions are simple functions. Now have a look at the following functions:

a) $f(x) = \sqrt{2x+6}$ b) $g(x) = \tan^3(3x + 5)$ c) $h(x) = e^{4x-7}$

The chain rule is a technique for finding the derivatives of composition functions, with the number of functions that make up the composition determining how many steps are necessary to reach the final solution.

Suppose a composition function f(x) is defined as:

$f(x) = (g.h)\ (x) = g[h(x)]$

then $f'(x) = g'[h(x)].h'(x)$

Let's take an example first.

Example 1: Find the differentiation of sin (log x).

Solution: Let $y = \sin(\log x)$

$d/dx(\sin \log x) = d(\sin \log x)/d(\log x) \times d(\log x)/dx = \cos(\log x)/x$

Here you can see that missing the loop will give you an incorrect answer, so it is important in the chain rule type of differentiation to observe each and every function minutely and differentiate accordingly.

In Vedic Mathematics this can be done by separating each

function and then differentiating them. The important point is to slice each function and write one below the other. On the right side of each function, write the differentiation. Finally club them together to get the answer.

Function	Differentiation
sin(log x)	cos(log x)
log x	1/x
Final answer	cos(log x)/x

Example 2: Find the derivative of sin (4x + 5).

Solution:

Function	Differentiation
sin(4x + 5)	cos(4x + 5)
4x + 5	4
Final answer	4cos(4x + 5)

Example 3: Find the derivative of $\log(\log(\log x^5)$.

Function	Differentiation
$\log(\log(\log x^5)$	$1/\log(\log x^5)$
$\log(\log x^5)$	$1/\log x^5 = 1/5 \log x$
$\log x^5$	$1/x^5$
x^5	$5x^4$

Hence, for $y = \log(\log(\log x^5)$

$$dy/dx = 5x^4/ x^5.5\log x.\log(\log x^5)$$

Example 4: Find the derivative of $\tan (\cos(\sin(\sqrt{x+6}).$

Solution:

Function	Differentiation
tan(cos(sin(√x+6)	sec²(cos(sin(√x+6)
(cos(sin(√x+6)	sin(sin(√x+6)
sin √x+6	cos(√x+6)
	1/2√x

Hence,

$$d/dx(\tan(\cos(\sin(\sqrt{x}+6)) = \frac{-\sec^2(\cos(\sin(\sqrt{x}+6) \times \sin(\sin(x \cos(\sqrt{x}+6))}{2\sqrt{x}}$$

Differentiation of the product of two functions

The derivative of the product of two different functions is generally obtained by applying the following formula:

$$d/dx(u.v) = u \, dv/dx + v \, du/dx$$

Example: Find the derivative of sin x.x⁴

Solution: Here we have two functions to differentiate

$$\frac{d(\sin x.x^4)}{dx} = x^4.\frac{d(\sin x)}{dx} + \sin x.\frac{d(x^4)}{dx}$$
$$= x^4\cos x + \sin x.4x^3$$

Example: Find the derivative of sin x.log x

Solution: Here we have two functions—trigonometric and logarithmic.

$$\frac{d(\sin x. \log x^4)}{dx} = \log x.\frac{d(\sin x)}{dx} + \sin x.\frac{d(\log x)}{dx}$$
$$= \log x.\cos x + \sin x.1/x$$

The whole operation involves the use of the simple formula of differentiation of the product of two functions. But what about doing these through a Vedic sutra? Here we shall use the Urdhva Tiryag sutra or the vertical and crosswise method to reach an answer.

Procedure:

- Write the two functions, one below the other, on the left hand side
- On the right side, write the differentiation of each function
- The final result is obtained by crosswise multiplication

Example 1: Find the derivative of $\sin^2 x.\log x$.

Solution:	Function	Differentiation

$$\sin^2 x \qquad\qquad 2\sin x.\cos x$$
$$\log x \qquad\qquad 1/x$$

$$\frac{d(\sin^2 x.\log x)}{dx} = \sin^2 x.1/x + 2\sin x.\cos x.\log x.$$

Example 2: Find the derivative of $e^x.\tan^{-1}x$.

Solution:	Function	Differentiation

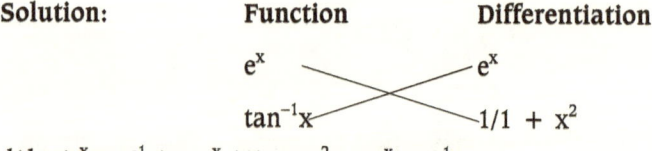

$$e^x \qquad\qquad e^x$$
$$\tan^{-1}x \qquad\qquad 1/1 + x^2$$

$$d/dx\ (e^x.\tan^{-1}x) = e^x.1/1 + x^2 + e^x.\tan^{-1}x$$

Example 3: Find the derivative of $x^5.\sin^3 x$

Solution:

Function	Differentiation
x^5	$5x^4$
sin^3x	$3sin^2x.cosx$

Hence, $d/dx (x^5.sin^3x) = x^5.3sin^2x.cos\ x + 5x^4.sin^3x$

Higher order derivatives

In higher order derivatives, we have to differentiate a function two, three, four times...and so on. Earlier we have used the symbols y_1, y_2, y_3...or y', y'', y''', but here we shall be using the symbols D_1, D_2, D_3...

Moreover, we have used the concept of the Pascal Triangle or **Meru Prastara** method to derive the final answer of the given function. In my book, *Mathematics and Religion*, I have provided detailed information about the Meru Prastara, better known as the Pascal triangle. Here we shall briefly deal with the Pascal triangle and then I shall explain the way it can be used to differentiate a function of a higher order.

```
                    1
                 1     1
              1     2     1
           1     3     3     1
        1     4     6     4     1
     1     5    10    10     5     1
  1     6    15    20    15     6     1
```

The Pascal triangle shown above is generally used in binomial expansion of different powers, and in my book, *Speed Mathematics*, you shall enjoy a complete chapter dedicated to the importance of the Pascal triangle. Now let's focus on its use in differentiating a function of a higher order.

Coefficients	Derivative
1 1	1st derivative – D_1
1 2 1	2nd derivative – D_2
1 3 3 1	3rd derivative – D_3
1 4 6 4 1	4th derivative – D_4
1 5 10 10 5 1	5th derivative – D_5

The procedure is as follows:

- First write the functions, one below the other.
- In their respective rows, write the differentiation of the given function as desired.
- Apply the vertical and crosswise rule and put a plus sign in between.
- Multiply each part of the answer with the coefficient as shown in the table.

How to do cross multiplication

a) For the first derivative

b) For the second derivative

c) For the third derivative

d) For the fourth derivative

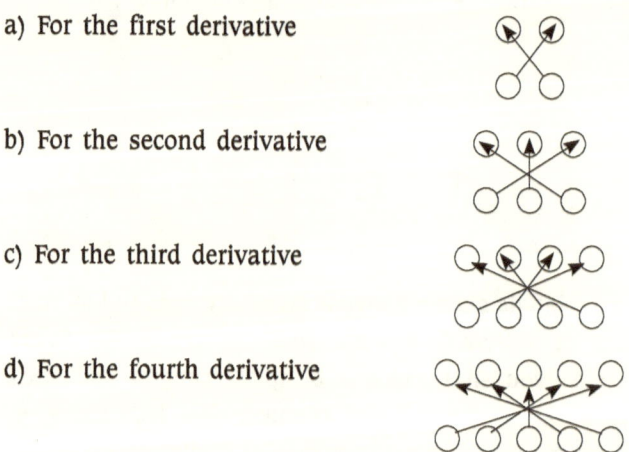

Example 1: Find the 1st, 2nd, 3rd and 4th derivatives of $x^5.\sin x$.

Solution: Let's begin with the 1st derivative.

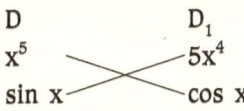

Coefficient   1   1

1st derivative = $1.x^5 \cos x + 1.\sin x.5x^4$

                 $= x^5\cos x + \sin x.5x^4$

For 2nd derivative

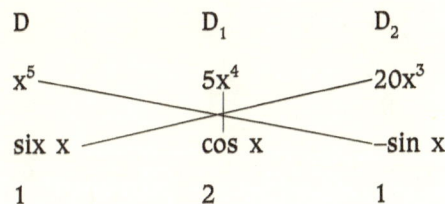

coefficient   1   2   1

2nd derivative = $x^5.\sin x + 2.5x^4.\cos x + 20x^3\sin x$

                 $= x^5.\sin x + 10x^4.\cos x + 20x^3\sin x$

For 3rd derivative

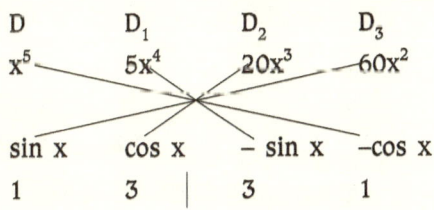

coefficient   1   3 | 3   1

Hence, 3rd derivative = $x^5\cos x + 3.5x^4.- \sin x + 3.20x^3.\cos x + 60x^2.\sin x$

     $= x^5\cos x.15x^4\sin x + 60\ x^3.\cos x + 60x^2.\sin x$

Example 2: Find the 1st, 2nd and 3rd derivative of $x^3 \cdot \sin x$.

Solution: 1st derivative

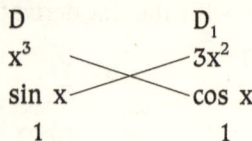

Coefficient   1   1

1st derivative $= x^3 \cos x + 3x^2 \sin x$

For 2nd derivative

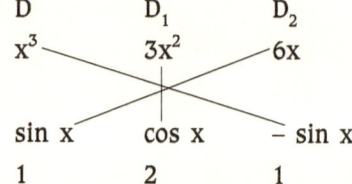

coefficient   1   2   1

Hence, 2nd derivative $= x^3 \sin x + 6x^2 \cos x + 6x \cdot \sin x$

For 3rd derivative

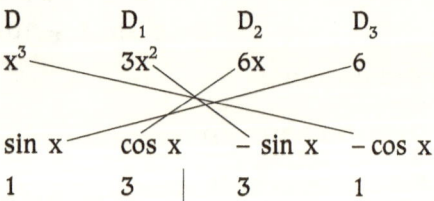

coefficient   1   3   3   1

Thus, 3rd derivative $= -x^3 \cos x - 9x^2 \sin x + 18 \cos x + 6 \sin x$

Simple differentiation, whether it is the product rule or the differentiation of any order, can be done with the help of the Vedic sutras Eknyun Purven or Anurupyen or Urdhva Tiryag (vertically and crosswise) through mere observation. But it requires practice as to how to place the coefficients of the Pascal triangle and write the final answers. Besides that, there is not much to do in simple differentiation as far as Vedic Mathematics is concerned. I do hope you will enjoy the Vedic method. I urge you to continue exploring the new technique.

16

Integration

Introduction

Integration is the reverse of differentiation. In differentiation, we have d/dx as the operator but here, the operator is $\int dx$. The dx inside the integration symbol means that integration is to be done with respect to x. There are two types of integration, definite integration and indefinite integration. Look at the following examples carefully:

If $y = 2x + 5$ then $dy/dx = 2$

If $y = 2x + 3$ then $dy/dx = 2$

If $y = 2x - 11$ then $dy/dx = 2$

In all the above examples we have seen that though the constant term in all the examples are different, the differentiation comes out to be the same. In the same way the integration of $\int 2dx = 2x + 5$, $2x + 3$ or $2x - 11$. Therefore, we add a constant at the end of the indefinite integration result.

Integration of power function

In differentiation we have seen that

$Y = x^6$, then $dy/dx = 6x^5$

$Y = x^{100}$ then $dy/dx = 100x^{99}$

Here we had used the method of Eknyun Purven, which means one less than the previous. In integration, we shall use Ekadhikena Purven or one more than the previous formula to integrate the power term of the function.

$\int x^n \, dx = \dfrac{1}{n+1} x^{n+1} + c$

$\int x^5 \, dx = x^6/6 + c \int 2x^9 \, dx = 2x^{10}/10 + c$

Here is a list of some trigonometric formulas.

$\int \sin x \, dx = -\cos x + c$

$\int \cos x \, dx = \sin x + c$

$\int \tan x \, dx = \log \sec x + c$

$\int \cot x \, dx = \log \sin x + c$

$\int \sec^2 x \, dx = \tan x + c$

$\int \operatorname{cosec}^2 x \, dx = -\cot x + c$

$\int \sec x \tan x \, dx = \sec x + c$

$\int \operatorname{cosec} x \cot x \, dx = -\operatorname{cosec} x + c$

$\int 1/x \, dx = \log x + c$

$\int e^x \, dx = e^x + c$

Besides that, there are several other formulas that we will look at in the meantime.

In case x is multiplied by some constant, the integrand function shall be divided by the same constant using the Vedic formula Anurupyen, which means 'proportionately'.

$$\int \cos 2x \, dx = \frac{\sin 2x}{2} + c$$

$$\int e^{4x+3} dx = \frac{e^{4x+3}}{4} + c$$

Vedic Mathematics is a powerful tool and is very effective if you have to do

a) Integration by parts
b) Partial fraction

Though the methods of substitution, successive integration, limit as a sum etc. are a few components of integration that can't be solved by the Vedic method effectively, the two most confusing areas of integration—integration by parts and integration using partial fraction—can be done through the Vedic sutra quite effectively and without error.

Integration of the sum or difference of functions

Integration of such functions is done by integrating each function separately and placing the respective sign in between.

Example 1: $\int x^3 + 6x + 7 \, dx$

Solution: $\int x^3 \, dx + 6 \int x \, dx + 7 \int dx$

$$= \frac{x^4}{4} + 6 \frac{x^2}{2} + 7x + c$$

Example 2: $\int \sin 2x + \sqrt{x} \, dx$

Solution: $\int \sin 2x \, dx + \int \sqrt{x} \, dx$

$$= \frac{-\cos 2x}{2} + \frac{x^{3/2}}{3/2} + c$$

Example 3: $\int x^7 + e^{2x} + x^a \, dx$

Solution: $\int x^7 \, dx + \int e^{2x} \, dx + \int x^a \, dx$

$$= \frac{x^8}{8} + \frac{e^{2x}}{2} + \frac{x^{a+1}}{a+1} + c$$

Example 4: $\int(\tan x + \sec^2 x)\, dx$

Solution: $\log \sec x + \tan x + c$

Integration by parts

We have seen how the differentiation of two different functions can be done using the product formula. Likewise, in integration, when we have to integrate the product of two different functions, we use the 'integration by parts' rule to solve such functions.

Typically, we follow the ILATE rule for selecting the first and second functions.

I = Inverse function – $\sin^{-1}x$
L = Logarithmic function – $\log x$
A = Algebraic function – x, y, z
T = Trigonometric function – $\sin x$, $\tan x$
E = Exponential Function – a^x, e^x

The formula we use to solve the question of integration by parts is –

$$\int uv\, dx = u\int v\, dx - \int \frac{du}{dx}\int(v\, dx)\, dx$$

The whole operation can be done in simple steps using Vedic Mathematics.

Procedure:

- Write the two functions, one below the other.
- Differentiate the first function and write the value adjacent to it.

- Integrate the second function and write it in front.
- Apply vertical and crosswise operation.
- The vertical operation involves the product of the differentiated and integrated value and will be applied if the integration of the term can be done easily, or else there will be successive differentiation of the first term and successive integration of the second term.
- The signs of the product are alternately positive and negative.

In simple words, in the Vedic method, one function is differentiated until zero is reached and the other function is integrated the same number of times. Integration by parts is basically the integration of the product of two functions. One function is differentiated as many times as needed till the final result comes out to be zero. The second function is also integrated as many times as needed till the differentiation is done.

$\int uv \, dx =$

u ... first function ... differentiation ... u^d

v ... second function ... integrated value ... v^i

u ... u^d

v ... v^i

$\int uv \, dx = uv^i - \int u^d.v^i \, dx$

Let's see some examples.

Example 1: $\int x \sin x \, dx$

Solution:

First function   x   1 −   Differentiation

Second function   sin x   − cos x   Integration

$$\int x \sin x \, dx = -x.\cos x - \int \cos x \, dx$$
$$= -x.\cos x + \sin x + c$$

Example 2: $\int x^4 . \cos x \, dx$

Solution:

First function x^4 $4x^3$ −   Differentiation

Second function   cox x   sin x   Integration

$$\int x^4 . \cos x \, dx = x^4 \sin x + \int 4x^3 \sin x \, dx$$

Since the second term under integration can be further integrated, we have to do successive differentiation and integration of each term.

Differentiation x^4 $4x^3$ $12x^2$ 24x   24

Integration   cos x   sin x   − cos x   − sin x   cos x

Sign   +   −   +   −   +

Hence, $\int x^4 . \cos x \, dx = x^4.\sin x + 4x^3\cos x - 12x^2\sin x - 24x. \cos x + \int 24\cos x \, dx$
$$= x^4.\sin x + 4x^3\cos x - 12x^2\sin x - 24x.\cos x + 24\sin x + c$$

Example 3: Integrate $\int x^3 . e^{2x} \, dx$

Solution:

First Function (Differentiation) x^3 $3x^2$ $6x$ 6 ↑

Second Function (Integration) e^{2x} $e^{2x}/2$ $e^{2x}/4$ $e^{2x}/8$

Sign + − + −

$\int x^3 . e^{2x} \, dx = x^3 . e^{2x}/2 - 3x^2 . e^{2x}/4 + 6x . e^{2x}/8 - \int \frac{6}{8} e^{2x} \, dx + c$

$= x^3 . e^{2x}/2 - 3x^2 . e^{2x}/4 + 6x . e^{2x}/8 - \int \frac{6}{8} \times \frac{1}{2} e^{2x} \, dx + c$

$x^3 . e^{2x}/2 - 3^{x2} . e^{2x}/4 + 6x . e^{2x}/8 - 3/8e^{2x} + c$

Integration by partial fraction

Integration of rational fractions can be done by using partial fractions, though solving a question by this method is understood to be one of the toughest jobs, as it involves a lot of calculations. However, in Vedic Mathematics, the same operation can be done in a single step and the answer can be reached in seconds.

Let's see how the same operation is done in the traditional method. Assume that we want to evaluate $\int \frac{P(x)}{Q(x)}$, where $\frac{P(x)}{Q(x)}$ is a proper rational function. In partial fractions, there will be decomposition of the integrand into a small and simpler fraction so as to reach an answer. Here are a few decompositions of a rational function.

Form of Rational Function	Form of Partial Function
$\dfrac{px + q}{(x - a)(x - b)}$	$\dfrac{A}{(x - a)} + \dfrac{A}{(x - b)}$

$\dfrac{px + q}{(x - a)^2}$	$\dfrac{A}{(x - a)} + \dfrac{A}{(x - b)^2}$
$\dfrac{px + q}{(x - a)(x^2 + b)}$	$\dfrac{A}{(x - a)} + \dfrac{Bx + c}{x^2 - b}$

Example 1: $\displaystyle \int \dfrac{dx}{(x + 1)(x + 2)}$

Solution: Let's solve it first using the method of partial fraction.

$$\dfrac{1}{(x + 1)(x + 2)} = \dfrac{A}{(x + 1)} + \dfrac{B}{(x + 2)}$$

where A and B are real numbers. On solving, we get

$1 = A(x + 2) + B(x + 1)$

$1 = x(A + B) + (2A + B)$

Equating the coefficients of equal terms, we get

$A + B = 0$ and $2A + B = 1$

On solving, we get $A = 1$ and $B = 1$

$$\dfrac{1}{(x + 1)(x + 2)} = \dfrac{1}{(x + 1)} + \dfrac{-1}{(x + 2)}$$

On integrating,

$$\int \dfrac{dx}{(x + 1)(x + 2)} = \int \dfrac{dx}{(x + 1)} - \int \dfrac{dx}{(x + 2)}$$

$$= \log |x + 1| \ \log |x + 2| + c$$

Now let's solve it using the technique of Vedic Mathematics.

$$\int \frac{dx}{(x + 1)(x + 2)}$$

First write the two rational functions with denominators as $(x + 1)$ and $(x + 2)$.

$$\int \frac{dx}{(x + 1)(x + 2)} = \int \frac{\square}{(x + 1)} + \frac{\square}{(x + 2)} \} dx$$

Now put the value of each denominator as equal to zero.

If $x + 1 = 0$ then $x = 1$ and if $x + 2 = 0$ then $x = 2$.

Since the first integration has $x + 1$ as denominator, put $x = 2$ in the first integrable function and $x = 1$ in the second integrable function. The result, thus obtained, has to be placed on the numerator of each integrable function.

$$\int \frac{dx}{(x + 1)(x + 2)} = \int \frac{\frac{1}{-1 + 2}}{x + 1} dx + \frac{\frac{1}{-2 + 1}}{x + 2} dx$$

$$= \int \frac{dx}{x + 1} - \int \frac{dx}{x + 2}$$

$$= \log |x + 1| - \log |x + 2| + c$$

Now you can imagine how easy it is to integrate using the Vedic method. Let me take more few examples.

Example 2: $\int \frac{2x}{(x + 1)(x + 2)} dx$

Solution: First, we need to write as many rational functions as the denominator has factors.

$$\int \frac{2x}{(x - 1)(x - 2)} dx = \int \frac{\square}{x - 1} + \int \frac{\square}{x - 2}$$

Since the first rational function has x − 1 in the denominator, put x − 1 = 0, giving x = 1. Put x = 1 in the integrable function omitting x − 1, and place the result in the numerator.

$$\int \frac{2x}{(x-1)\ (x-2)}\ dx = \int \frac{\frac{2 \times 1}{(1-2)}}{x-1}\ dx + \int \frac{\boxed{}}{x-2}\ dx$$

The second rational function has x − 2 in the denominator, so put x = 2 in the original integrable function omitting x − 2, and place it in the numerator of the second integrable function.

$$\int \frac{2x}{(x-1)\ (x+2)}\ dx = \int \frac{\frac{2 \times 1}{(1-2)}}{x+1}\ dx + \int \frac{\frac{2 \times 2}{(2-1)}}{x-1}\ dx$$

$$= \int \frac{-2}{x+1}\ dx + \int \frac{4}{x-2}\ dx$$

$$= -2 \log |x-1| + 4 \log |x-2| + c$$

Example 3: $\int \dfrac{3x-1}{(x+1)\ (x+2)\ (x+3)}\ dx$

Solution:

$$\int \frac{3x-1}{(x-1)\ (x-2)\ (x-3)}\ dx = \int \frac{\boxed{}}{x-1}\ dx = \int \frac{\boxed{}}{x-2}\ dx + \int \frac{\boxed{}}{x-3}\ dx$$

$$= \int \frac{\frac{3 \times 1-1}{(1-2)\ (1-3)}}{(x-1)}\ dx = \int \frac{\frac{3 \times 1-1}{(1-2)\ (1-3)}}{(x-1)}\ dx + \int \frac{\frac{3 \times 3-1}{(3-1)\ (3-2)}}{(x-3)}\ dx$$

$$= \int \frac{1}{x-1}\ dx + \int \frac{-5}{x-2}\ dx + \int \frac{4}{x-3}\ dx$$

$$= \log |x-1| - 5 \log |x-2| + 4 \log| x-3| + c$$

Example 4: $\int \dfrac{x^2}{(x^2-2)\ (x^2+3)}\ dx$

Solution:

$$\int \frac{x^2}{(x^2-2)\,(x^2+3)}\,dx = \int \frac{\square}{(x^2-2)}\,dx + \int \frac{\square}{(x^2+3)}\,dx$$

Since $x^2 - 2 = 0$ gives $x^2 = 2$, place $x^2 = 2$ in the given rational function and place the value in the numerator part of the first integrable function. Don't forget to omit $x^2 - 2$ from the denominator as it will make the rational function invalid. Follow the same for the second integrable function.

$$\int \frac{x^2}{(x^2-2)\,(x^2+3)}\,dx = \int \frac{\dfrac{2}{(2+3)}}{(x^2-2)}\,dx + \int \frac{\dfrac{-3}{-3-2}}{(x^2-3)}\,dx$$

$$= 2/5 \int \frac{\overset{u}{1}}{(x^2-2)}\,dx + 3/5 \int \frac{1}{(x^2+3)}\,dx$$

$$= 2/5\left\{ \frac{1}{2\sqrt{2}} \log \frac{x-\sqrt{2}}{x+\sqrt{2}} + \frac{3}{5} \times \frac{1}{\sqrt{3}} \tan^{-1} \frac{x}{\sqrt{3}} + c \right.$$

Example: $\int \sin\theta \, \cos\theta/(4\sin\theta - 1)\,(2\sin\theta + 1)\,d\theta$

Solution: Put $\sin\theta = u$

On differentiating with respect to θ, we get $\cos\theta \, d\theta = du$
Hence, the integrable function changes to

$$\int \frac{u\,du}{(4u-1)\,(2u+1)}$$

$$= \int \frac{u\,du}{(4u-1)\,(2u+1)} = \int \frac{\square}{4u-1}\,du + \int \frac{\square}{2u+1}\,du$$

Put $4u - 1 = 0$ and $2u + 1 = 0$ and place the result obtained in the respective numerators on the right side, omitting the factor in each rational function integrable so that the denominator doesn't become zero.

$$= \int \frac{\frac{1}{4}}{\frac{2 \times \frac{1}{4} + 1}{4u - 1}} du + \int \frac{-\frac{1}{2}}{\frac{4 \times -\frac{1}{2} - 1}{2u + 1}} du$$

$$= \frac{1}{6} \int \frac{du}{4u - 1} + \frac{1}{6} \int \frac{du}{2u + 1}$$

$$= 1/24 \log |4u - 1| + 1/12 \log |2u + 1| + c$$

$$= 1/24 \log |4\sin\theta - 1| + 1/12 \log |4\sin\theta + 1| + c$$

I hope you have enjoyed integration by the Vedic method. It saves your time and the chances of getting it wrong are less as you omit the tough method of partial fraction practised in schools, and apply this simple and lucid method to solve even the most cumbersome integration in a few steps.

17

Trigonometry

Introduction

In a right-angled triangle, the ratio between two sides is calculated using trigonometry. The concept of trigonometry is first introduced in the secondary level, where you are required to find the ratio of two sides with some given data. Sometimes you find angles between two consecutive sides.

Do you remember the first day of trigonometry class, when the teacher wrote:

Some people have curly brown hair turned permanently black?

Here S = Sine, P = Perpendicular, H = Hypotenuse, C = Cosine, B = Base and T = Tangent

This is remembered in the funniest ways, like:

Sine	Cosine	Tangent
Pandit	Badri	Prasad
Hari	Hari	Bole

where Sine of an angle = Perpendicular/Hypotenuse

Cosine of an angle = Base/Hypotenuse

Tangent of an angle = Perpendicular/Base

However, at the senior secondary level, we learn to find the value of multiple and sub-multiple angles, and in doing so, we are forced to memorize scores of formulae.

Let me remind you of the following concepts of trigonometry, which you have learnt at the secondary level. In a right-angled triangle, ABC, with angle C = 90°, the various trigonometric ratios are defined as follows:

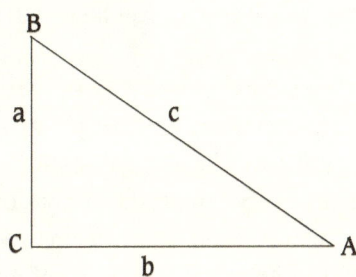

Trigonometric Ratio	Value	Vedic Triple Case
Sin A	a/c	1st value/3rd value
Cos A	b/c	2nd value/3rd value
Tan A	a/b	1st value/2nd value
Cot A	b/a	2nd value/1st value
Sec A	c/b	3rd value/2nd value
Cosec A	c/a	3rd value/1st value

In the above table, the sides a, b and c are taken as a triple. You must remember the Pythagoras Theorem, which states: in a right-angle triangle, the square of the hypotenuse is equal to the sum of the squares of the other two sides.

$$\text{Hypotenuse}^2 = \text{Perpendicular}^2 + \text{Base}^2$$
$$c^2 = a^2 + b^2$$

Do you know that the Pythagoras Theorem was discovered long before Pythagoras was born? In the Sulva sutra written in the 8th–6th century BC, you can find references to the Pythagoras Theorem. Some people credit it to Baudhayana. The ancient mathematician used to apply deep geometrical concepts, but the purpose of using geometry was purely pious. While constructing an altar for worship, they would measure with sulva (rope) and construct an altar in the shape of right-angled triangles, rectangles, squares, etc.

Let's see what the western scholars had to state about the Pythagoras Theorem.

François-Marie Arouet (1694–1774), better known as Voltaire, wrote, 'I am convinced that everything has come down to us from the banks of the Ganga—astronomy, astrology, spiritualism, etc. It is very important to note that 2500 years ago at least Pythagoras went from Samos to the Ganga to learn geometry … But he would certainly not have undertaken such a strange journey had the reputation of the Brahmins' science not been long established in Europe.'[1]

Professor H.G. Rawlinson wrote, 'It is more likely that Pythagoras was influenced by India than by Egypt. Almost all the theories, religions, philosophical and mathematical, taught by the Pythagoreans, were known in India in the sixth century B.C., and the Pythagoreans, like the Jains and the Buddhists, refrained from the destruction of life and eating meat and regarded certain vegetables such as beans as taboo. It seems that the so-called Pythagorean Theorem of the quadrature of the hypotenuse was already known to the Indians in the older

---

[1]N. Krishnaswamy and Harini Narayan, 'Observations of the World's Great Minds on the Indian Heritage', The Vedic Way of Life for the First Time Reader, 2014, p 70. http://www.vidyavrikshah.org/THEVEDICWAYOFLIFE.pdf

Vedic times, and thus, before Pythagoras.[2]

Even in Sulva sutra, you will find references to the triples. The triple is the relation between all the three sides of a right-angled triangle. If perpendicular = 3 units, base = 4 units then,

$$\text{Hypotenuse} = \sqrt{\text{Perpendicular}^2 + \text{Base}^2} = 5$$

So, (3, 4, 5) is the primary triple. It means all the three sides are related via a special condition. In order to get faster calculations in Vedic Mathematics, you need to memorize the Pythagorean triple. Here is a table to help you.

A	B	C
3	4	5
5	12	13
6	8	10
7	24	25
8	15	17
9	40	41
9	12	15
10	24	26
11	60	61
12	15	18
3n	4n	5n

For more information on geometry during the Vedic period, you could refer to my book, *Mathematics in Religion*. To find the value of some angles, you may refer to my book *Maths Made Easy*.

---

[2] 'Mathematics', Hindu Online,
http://hinduonline.co/FactsAboutHinduism/Mathematics.html

Computing trigonometric ratio

Let us suppose you are given the following example to solve.

Example: If tan A = 8/15, find the value of other trigonometric ratios.

The traditional method will use a different formula to arrive at the result.

$$\cot A = 1/\tan A = 15/8$$

$$\sec^2 A = 1 + \tan^2 A = 1 + 64/225 = 289/225,$$
$$\text{so sec A} = 17/15$$

$$\cos A = 1/\sec A = 15/17$$

$$\sin^2 A = 1 - \cos^2 A = 1 - 225/289 = 64/289,$$
$$\text{so sin A} = 8/17$$

$$\csc A = 1/\sin A = 17/8$$

Now let us see how the triple helps us to compute the values of other trigonometric ratios. From the above table on triples, you can find the missing triple if:

a = 8   b = 15   then   c = 17

Now move to the trigonometric table and find the value of other trigonometric ratios in no time.

$$\sin A = a/c = 8/17$$
$$\cos A = b/c = 15/17$$

The other ratios can be easily found, as cosec A is the inverse of sin A and sec A is the inverse of cos A.

Take another example.

Example: If cosec A = 61/11, find tan A.

By the Pythagorean triple, the third number in the series of 11, 61...is obviously 60.

Since sin A = 1/cosec A = 11/61 = first value/third value

a = 11, c = 61, therefore b = 60

Now from the trigonometric table given above,

tan A = first value/second value = a/b = 11/60

The above examples are enough to prove that the triple method of Vedic Mathematics is interesting, easy to understand and time-saving. Now, let us extend the value to twice the angle.

Computing trigonometric ratio of twice the angle (2A)

As discussed above, the triple for angle A is – a, b and c. On extending the result for twice the angle i.e. 2A, we can find that the triples for the angle 2A are $2ab$, $b^2 - a^2$ and c^2.

Let us look at an example.

If sin A = 3/5, find tan 2A.

Traditional method:

We have $\cos^2 A = 1 - \sin^2 A$

$$= 1 - 9/25 = 16/25$$

$$\cos A = 4/5$$

Moreover, tan A = sin A/cos A

So, tan A = 3/4

Hence tan 2A = 2 tan A/1 + $\tan^2 A$

$$= \frac{2 \times 3/4}{1 - (3/4)^2} = 24/7$$

Now let's view the problem through the Vedic triple method.

We have sin A = 3/5

Here a = 3 and c = 5, so obviously b = 4 (see triple table).

Now make the triple for twice the angle, i.e. for 2A.

The triples are:

$2ab$	$b^2 - a^2$	and	c^2
$2 \times 3 \times 4$	$4^2 - 3^2$		5^2
24	7		25

Hence,

tan 2A = 1st value/2nd value = 24/7.

Example: If cos A = 9/41, find cos 2A.

Solution: First find the triple for angle A.

cos A = 2nd value/3rd value = b/c

Hence, the missing triple a = 40.

So we have a = 40,   b = 9 and c = 41.

Now the triples for 2A are:

2ab,	$b^2 - a^2$	and	c^2
$2 \times 40 \times 9$,	$40^2 - 9^2$,		41^2
720	1519		1681

So,

cos 2A = 2nd value/3rd value = 1519/1681.

Computing trigonometric relation for thrice the angle (3A)

We have so far seen the triples for angles A and 2A. Let's extend it for 3A to find the value of sin 3A, cos 3A and tan 3A.

The triples for 3A are:

$$3ac^2 - 4a^3, \qquad 4b^3 - 3bc^2 \quad \text{and} \qquad c^3$$

Example:

If tan A = 7/24, find sin 3A and cos 3A.

Solution: The triple for angle A:

tan A = 7/24 = 1st value/2nd value

Hence, the missing part of the triple = 25 = 3rd value, i.e. a = 7, b = 24 and c = 25

Let us find the value of the triple for angle 3A.

The triples are:

$3ac^2 - 4a^3$, $4b^3 - 3bc^2$ and c^3

$3 \times 7 \times 252 - 4 \times 7^3$, $4 \times 24^3 - 3 \times 24 \times 25^2$, 25^3

11753   10296   15625

(For square and cube of a number, refer to the respective chapters.)

Hence sin 3A = 1st value/3rd value = 11753/15625

cos 3A = 2nd value/3rd value = 10296/15625.

Computing trigonometric relation for half the angle (A/2)

If the triples for the angle A are a, b and c, then the triples for A/2 are:

$$a, \qquad b + c \quad \text{and} \quad \sqrt{(b + c)^2 + a^2}$$

Example: If sin A = 12/13, find the value of tan A/2.

Solution: We have, sin A = 1st value/3rd value

Here, a = 12, c = 13 therefore from the triple table b = 5.
Now find the triple for A/2.

a,	b + c	and	$\sqrt{(b + c)^2 + a^2}$
12	5 + 13		$\sqrt{18^2 + 12^2}$
12	18		$\sqrt{468}$
12	18		$6\sqrt{13}$

Hence tan A/2 = 1st value/2nd value = $12/6\sqrt{13} = 2/\sqrt{13}$

Now let us summarize the triple in the given table.

Angle	a	b	c
A	a	b	c
2A	2 ab	$b^2 - a^2$	c^2

3A	$3ac^2 - 4a^3$	$4b^3 - 3bc^2$	c^3
A/2	a	$b + c$	$\sqrt{(b + c)^2 + a^2}$

The above table will help you immensely to find the different trigonometric ratios with ease, and thus save you precious time. Once you are well equipped with the methods of finding the square and cube, you can do the calculations involved in sin 3A, cos 2A etc. quite easily.

Sum of angles using triples

We do have the following two formulas which help us to find the sum of angles in trigonometry.

sin(A + B) = sin Acos B + cos Asin B

cos(A + B) = cos Acos B – sin Asin B

The main area of concern when using this formula is if we are given sin A = 8/17 and cos B = 3/5, and asked to find the values of sin(A + B) and cos(A + B).

We have to first find the values of cos A and sin B and then substitute in the above formula, and after some calculations we will be able to get the answer. If you remember the triple then it will hardly take a minute to find the values of sin(A + B) and cos(A + B).

If the triple of angle A is x, y, z and triple for B is X, Y and Z, then the triple for the angle A + B is given by:

A	x	y	z
B	X	Y	Z
A + B	yX + xY	yY – xX	zZ

This can be better understood using the Dot and Cross method.

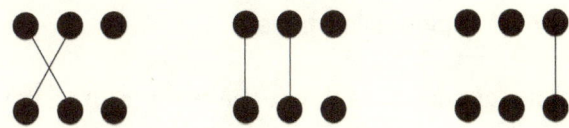

Example 1: If sin A = 3/5 and sin B = 8/17, then find the value of sin(A + B) and cos(A + B).

Solution: Let us first draw the triple table for the angles A and B.

A	3	4	5
B	8	15	17
A + B	3 × 15 + 4 × 8 = 77	4 × 15 − 3 × 8 = 36	5 × 17 = 85

Hence, sin(A + B) = 77/85

cos(A + B) = 36/85

Example 2: If sin A = 7/25 and sin B = 8/17 then find the value of sin(A + B) and cos(A + B).

Solution: Let us first draw the triple table for the angles A and B.

A	7	24	25
B	8	15	17
A + B	7 × 15 + 24 × 8 = 297	24 × 15 − 7 × 8 = 304	25 × 17 = 425

Hence, sin(A + B) = 297/425

cos(A + B) = 304/425

Difference of angles using triples

If the triple for angle A is x, y, z and triple for B is X, Y and Z then the triple for the angle A + B is given by:

A	x	y	z
B	X	Y	Z
A − B	xY − Xy	xX + yY	zZ

This can be better understood using the Dot and Cross method.

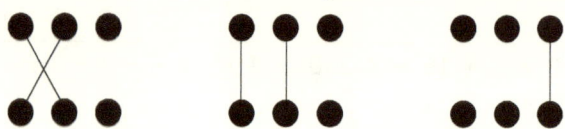

Example 1: If sin A = 7/25 and sin B = 8/17 then find the value of sin (A − B) and cos (A − B).

Solution: Let us first draw the triple table for the angles A and B.

A	7	24	25
B	8	15	17
A − B	7 × 15 − 24 × 8 = − 77	24 × 15 + 7 × 8 = 416	25 × 17 = 425

Hence, sin(A − B) = − 77/425

cos(A − B) = 416/425

If a triple has a negative sign then obviously the angle is obtuse.

Example 2: If sin A = 3/5 and sin B = 8/17 then find the value of sin(A − B) and cos(A − B).

Solution: Let us first draw the triple table for the angles A and B.

A	3	4	5
B	8	15	17
A − B	$3 \times 15 - 4 \times 8$	$4 \times 15 + 3 \times 8$	5×17
	$= 13$	$= 84$	$= 85$

Hence, $\sin(A - B) = 13/85$

$\cos(A - B) = 84/85$

Triples are very useful in finding the compound angles (A + B), (A − B)...and also angles above 90 degrees. Please refer to *Maths Made Easy* to study the concept in detail.

18

Casting-out-nines Method

Introduction

Casting-out-nines or **Navansh** method is the most effective tool used in Vedic Mathematics. Though this is not a foolproof method, it is certainly the best method to check all the eight fundamental operations used in mathematics. Here I am talking about addition, subtraction, multiplication, division, square, square root, cube and cube root. This method in mathematics is also as popular as the Chinese remainder theorem, but as you all know, the whole world is indebted to the Indian numeral system. It is not known as to how and why it was credited to the Chinese. Laplace wrote,

> The ingenious method of expressing every possible number using a set of ten symbols (each symbol having a place value and an absolute value) emerged in India. The idea seems so simple nowadays that its significance and profound importance is no longer appreciated. Its simplicity lies in the way it facilitated calculation and placed arithmetic foremost amongst useful inventions. The importance of this invention is more readily appreciated when one considers that

it was beyond the two greatest men of antiquity, Archimedes and Apollonius.[1]

Let me explain why I am a great fan of this method.

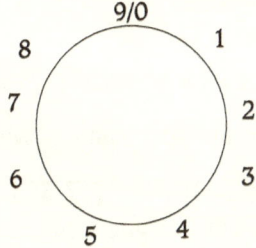

The nine numbers placed on the circle are the best example to understand this method. Look at the circle. Here I have put 9 and 0 side by side. As the name suggests, Casting-out-nines means you simply have to throw out 9 wherever you get it. It is more interesting to note that if you sum up the digits of a number, however large it is, you will always get a single digit sum between 1 and 9. Let's begin with a two-digit number.

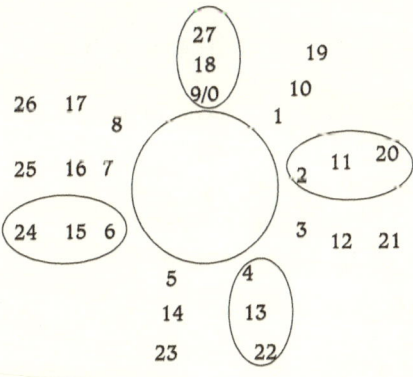

---

[1]H. Eves, Return to Mathematical Circles, Boston: Prindle, Weber and Schmidt, 1988.

The digit sums of 2, 11, 20, 29...or 4, 13, 22...or 6, 15, 24... are the same. This clearly shows that for any number you take, the final sum is within 1 to 9, if 9 is removed or if 0 and 9 are considered to be the same for a while.

Example 1:

Find the digit sum of 2456819873487298373727235570804.

Solution: First strike out the numbers whose sum is 9.

2 ~~45~~ 6 ~~81~~ ~~9~~ ~~873~~ 48 ~~72~~ ~~9~~ ~~837~~ ~~372~~ ~~72~~ 3570804

Here the digit 9, sum of the digits reaching 9 and its multiples 18, 27...etc. have been struck out. Now add the left out digits.

$2 + 6 + 4 + 8 + 3 + 3 + 5 + 7 + 0 + 8 + 0 + 4 = 50$

Digit sum of $50 = 5 + 0 = 5$

Hence, digit sum of

2 ~~45~~ 6 ~~81~~ ~~9~~ ~~873~~ 48 ~~72~~ ~~9~~ ~~837~~ ~~372~~ ~~72~~ 3570804 is 5.

Example 2: Find the digit sum of 4379348568219.

Solution: Add all the digits.

4 3 7 ~~9~~ 3 4 8 5 6 8 2 1 ~~9~~

The four groups of numbers have the digit sum 9 which need not be taken into account.

Hence the final sum = digits left out

$= 4 + 3 + 8 = 15$

Digit sum of $15 = 1 + 5 = 6$

Example 3: Find the digit sum of 4780926782.

Solution: Add all the digits.

4 7 8 0 ~~9~~ 2 6 7 8 2

Digit sum of left out numbers = 4 + 8 + 6 + 8 = 8 as the sum of 4 + 8 + 6 = 18 is a multiple of 9.

In fact, digit sums 9 and 0 are equivalent, and the nine-point circle points towards the same. Therefore, you can strike out both 9 and 0 to calculate the digit sum of the given number. In Vedic Mathematics we have a sutra—Sunyam Sama Samuccaye, which means when the samuccaye is same, it is zero. This is interesting, as the digit sum of 456 is the same as 6. The digit sum of 45 is 4 + 5 = 9, so digit sum of 456 is 6.

Let's see how this method is used to check the fundamental operations in mathematics.

Checking addition

Example 1: Check if 76 + 88 = 154

Solution: Digit sum of 76 = 7 + 6 = 13; 1 + 3 = 4
Digit sum of 88 = 8 + 8 = 16; 1 + 6 = 7
Digit sum for 76 + 88 = 4 + 7 = 11; 1 + 1 = 2
Digit sum of 154 = 1 + (5 + 4) = 1
Since Digit sum of 76 + 88 ≠ Digit sum of 154
Hence, the addition is incorrect.

Example 2: Check if 47892 + 6256 + 34967 = 89115.

Solution:

	Digit sum	
47892	3 ⎫	
6256	1 ⎬ Sum of Digit Sum = 3 + 1 + 2 = 6	
34967	2 ⎭	
89115	6	

Example 3: Check 54987 + 35648 + 35910 = 127545

Solution: First write the digit sum of each of the numbers adjacent to the number.

Digit sum of 54987   = 6 ⎫
Digit sum of 35648   = 8 ⎪ Sum of these digit sums = 6
Digit sum of 35910   = 0 ⎬ + 8 + 0 = 14; 1 + 4 = 5
Digit sum of 127545   = 6 ⎭

Since digit sum of LHS ≠ Digit sum of RHS, the addition is incorrect.

Checking subtraction

Example 1: 645879 – 32589 = 613,290

Solution: Digit sum of 645879 = 3

Digit sum of 32589   = 0 ⎫ Difference of digit sum =
Digit Sum of 613,290 = 3 ⎭ 3 – 0 = 3

Since Digit sum of LHS = Digit sum of RHS,
    the calculation is right.

Example 2: Check 5896245 – 4597862 = 1296383

Solution: Digit sum of 5896245 = 3

$$\frac{\text{Digit sum of } 4597862 = 5}{\text{Difference of digit sum} = 3 - 5 = -2}$$

In case you have a negative sign at the end of the operation, add 9 to it to make it positive.

    Difference of digit sum = – 2 + 9 = 7
    Digit sum of 1296383 = 5

Since Digit sum of LHS = Digit sum of RHS, the answer is wrong.

N.B.: It is not always necessary to convert the negative sign into positive by adding 9. In the above example, you have seen that $3 - 5 = -2$ can be written as $12 - 5 = 7$ or $21 - 5 = 16$ and digit sum of $16 = 7$

Digit sum of 12 = Digit sum of 21 = Digit sum of 30 = 3

Checking multiplication

The method discussed so far is equally applicable for multiplication.

Example 1: Check $123 \times 324 = 39852$

Solution: Digit sum of 123 = 6
Digit sum of 324 = 0
Product of digit sum = $6 \times 0 = 0$
Digit sum of 39852 = 0
Hence, calculation is correct.

Example 2: Check $67589 \times 5478 = 370241542$

Solution: Digit sum of 67589 = 8
Digit sum of 5478 = 6
Product of digit sum = $8 \times 6 = 48$ and its digit sum = 3
Digit sum of final result = $3 + 7 + 0 + 2 + 4 + 1 + 5 + 4 + 2 = 1$
Since digit sum of LHS $\neq$ Digit sum of RHS
Therefore, calculation is incorrect.

Checking division

In division you need to learn the basic formula used to check the answer.

Dividend = Divisor x Quotient + Remainder

Find the digit sum of each of the terms and place it in the formula to check the final result.

Example 1: Verify 287695 / 3456, Q = 83 and R = 847

Solution:

Here dividend = 287695

Digit sum of dividend = 2 + 8 + 7 +6 + 9 + 5 = 1

Divisor = 3456

Digit sum of divisor = 3 + 4 + 5 + 6 = 0

Quotient = 83

Digit sum of quotient = 8 + 3 = 2

Remainder = 847

Digit sum of remainder = 8 + 4 + 7 = 1

Putting the digit sum value in the given formulae, we get,

LHS = Digit sum of Dividend = 1

RHS = Divisor × Quotient + Remainder

= 0 × 2 + 1 = 1

Hence LHS = RHS

Therefore, the result is verified.

Example 2: Check 352 / 13; Q = 27, R = 2

Solution: Dividend = 352

Digit sum of 352 = 1

Divisor = 13

Digit sum of 13 = 4

Quotient = 27

Digit sum of 27 = 0
Remainder = 2
Place these values in the given formula
RHS = Divisor × Quotient + Remainder
  = 4 × 0 + 2 = 2
LHS = Dividend = 1
Since LHS ≠ RHS
Therefore, result is incorrect.

Checking calculations having multiple operations

Example 1: Check 2457 − 1298 + 8761 − 7654 = 2266

Solution: Get the digit sum of each number and place it below the number to check whether the result obtained on the LHS is the same as that of the digit sum of the RHS.

Digit sum of 2457 = 0
Digit sum of 1298 = 2
Digit sum of 8761 = 4
Digit sum of 7654 = 4
LHS = 2457 − 1298 + 8761 − 7654
    = 0 − 2 + 4 − 4 = − 2
Make the LHS positive by adding 9
Hence the corrected LHS = 7
Digit sum of RHS = 2 + 2 + 6 + 6 = 7
Here, Digit sum of LHS = Digit sum of RHS
Hence, the result is correct.

Example 2: 8294 × 123 − 65321 + 7654 − 82761 = 872080
Digit sum of 8294 = 5
Digit sum of 123 = 6
Digit sum of 65321 = 8

Digit sum of 7654 = 4

Digit sum of 82761 = 6

LHS = 8294 × 123 – 65321 + 7654 – 82761

= 5 × 6 – 8 + 4 – 6 = 20

Digit sum of LHS = 2

RHS = 872080

Digit sum of 872080 = 7

Since LHS ≠ RHS calculation is incorrect.

Example 3: 12 × 13 + 5698 + 12167 ÷ 23 – 6142 = 241

Solution: In such examples, we need to follow the BODMAS trick and apply the digit sum method to check the result.

Let's begin.

DS of 12 = 3

DS of 13 = 4

DS of 5698 = 1

DS of 12167 = 8

DS of 23 = 5

DS of 6142 = 4

DS of 241 = 7

Now place the digit sum at the required place.

LHS = 12 × 13 + 5698 + 12167 ÷ 23 – 6142

= 3 × 4 + 1 + 8 ÷ 5 – 4

= 12 + 1 + 1.6 – 4

= 14. 6 – 4 = 10.6

DS of 10.6 = 7

RHS = DS of 241 = 7

Since DS of LHS = DS of RHS calculation is correct.

As the examples suggest, the casting-out-nines method is useful in checking different operations at a time. The beauty of this method can be best enjoyed if in a competitive examination, you have four options with different operations in a single question. Then you can check the answer with the help of this method and hit the bullseye.

Now where the square/cube of a number is concerned, it is basically multiplying a particular number by itself, twice or thrice.

Cube of $12 = 12 \times 12 \times 12$

Square of $12 = 12 \times 12$

The same digit sum method will be applicable here.

Checking squares

Look at the following table:

Number	1	2	3	4	5	6	7	8	9
Square	1	4	9	16	25	36	49	64	81
DS	1	4	0	7	7	0	4	1	0

The minute observation of the table suggests that the DS of (1, 8), (2, 7), (3, 6) and (4, 5) are the same. So, you need to remember only four DS values to check the square calculation.

Example 1: Verify $(106)^2 = 12336$

Solution:

LHS = Digital sum of $(106)^2 = (1 + 0 + 6)^2 = 4$

RHS = Digital sum of $12336 = 1 + 2 + 3 + 3 + 6 = 7$

LHS $\neq$ RHS

Therefore, the result is incorrect.

Example 2: Verify $(938)^2 = 879834$

Solution:

LHS = Digital sum of $(938)^2 = (9 + 3 + 8)2 = $ DS of $(11)^2$
$= 4$

RHS = Digital sum of 879834 = 8 + 7 + 9 + 8 + 3 + 4 = 3
LHS ≠ RHS

Therefore, the result is incorrect.

The square root can be checked by the reverse process. We know that $(2)^2 = \sqrt{4}$ but = 2 (taking only the positive sign). So, to check the square root we need to take the reverse order.

Example 3: $\sqrt{4225} = 65$?

Solution: $\sqrt{\text{DS of } 4225} = 2$

DS of 65 = 2

Therefore, the result is correct.

Otherwise, you can change the operation like:

$(65)^2 = 4225$

DS of $(65)^2 = (2)^2 = 4$

DS of 4225 = 4

Therefore, the result is correct.

Checking cubes

Look at the following table and notice the pattern.

Number	1	2	3	4	5	6	7	8	9
Cube	1	8	27	64	125	216	343	512	729
Digit Sum	1	8	0	1	8	0	1	8	0

The digit sums of the cubes of 1, 4 and 7 are the same, similarly the digit sums of the cubes of 2, 5 and 8 are the same. In the same way, the digit sums of 3, 6 and 9 are the same.

Let's understand the fact with some examples.

Example 1: Is $(12)^3 = 1742$?

Solution: DS of 12 is 3

DS of $(12)^3 = (3)^3 = 0$

DS of result $= 1 + 7 + 4 + 2 = 5$

Hence, the result is incorrect.

Example 2: Verify $(928)^3 = 799168552$

Solution:

LHS $=$ Digital sum of $(928)^2 = (9 + 2 + 8)^3 = (10)^3 = 1$

RHS $=$ Digital sum of $799168552 = 7 + 9 + 9 + 1 + 6 + 8 + 5 + 5 + 2 = 7$

LHS $\neq$ RHS

Therefore the result is incorrect.

In the same way, you can check the calculations for cube roots. This is the easiest method for checking the fundamental operation, so you must keep calculating and checking in order to achieve proficiency in the Casting-out-nines method.

Practice Questions

HCF of Polynomials

Find the HCFs of the following polynomials.

a) $3m^3 - 12m^2 + 21m - 18$ and $6m^3 - 30m^2 + 60m - 48$

b) $a^3 + 2a^2 - 3a$ and $2a^3 + 5a^2 - 3a$

c) $m^2 + 9m + 20$ and $m^2 + 13m + 36$

d) $x^3 - 9x^2 + 23x - 15$ and $4x^2 - 16x + 12$

e) $3x^3 + 18x^2 + 33x + 18$ and $3x^2 + 13x + 10$

f) $2x^3 + 2x^2 + 2x + 2$ and $6x^3 + 12x^2 + 6x + 12$

Differentiation

Find the derivatives of the following.

a) $x^2\cos x$

b) $\sin^3 x.\cos^3 x$

c) $(3x + 5)(1 + \tan x)$

d) $(\sec x - 1)(\sec x + 1)$

e) $y = (6x^2 + 7x)^4$

f) $2\sin(3x + \tan(x))$

g) Find the first, second, and third derivatives of
$f(x) = 5x^4 - 3x^3 + 7x^2 - 9x + 2$

h) Find the first, second, and third derivatives of $y = \sin 2x$

Division of polynomials

1. Divide $6x^2 + x - 15$ by $2x - 3$
2. Divide $x^3 - 3x^2 - 10x + 24$ by $x - 4$
3. Divide $2y^3 + 6y^2 + 12y + 8$ by $y + 1$
4. Divide $x^3 + x^2 - 8x - 12$ by $x - 3$
5. Divide $a^2 + 8$ by $a + 2$
6. Divide $12m^2 - m - 17$ by $3m + 2$

Combined operations

1. $345 \times 653 + 234 \times 16 - 123 \times 54$
2. $12346 + 78530 - 4387 - 5297$
3. $23 \times 67 + 45 \times 92 - 34 \times 69$
4. $23 \times 99 + 1052 - 34 \times 86$
5. $876 + 987321 - 76985 + 1456 \times 32 - 341 \times 89$
6. $192 + 462 - 562 - 172 + 1000$

Cubing

Find the cubes of the following using the appropriate Vedic sutra and check the result by the Casting-out-nines method.

a) 98   b) 23   c) 42   d) 107 e) 992 f) 125   g) 214

Squaring

Find the squares of the following using the appropriate Vedic sutra and check the result by the Casting-out-nines method.

a) 425 b) 3287 c) 19   d) 291 e) 113 f) 994 g) 37 h) 337

Multiplication of polynomials

a) $(2x + 3y) \times (4x + 7y)$

b) $(a + 7z) \times (2a + 11z)$

c) $(x^2 + 4z) \times (9x^2 + 7z)$

d) $(2x^2 + 4x + 7) \times (x^2 + 7x - 9)$

e) $(5x^2 - 9x - 8) \times (4x^2 - 7x + 8)$

f) $(7x^2 - 6x) \times (x^2 - 3x + 4)$

g) $(12x^2 - 7x) \times (3x + 4)$

h) $(8x^2 + 4) \times (7x^2 + 2x + 5)$

i) $(4x + 7y) \times (2x + 6y)$

j) $(2a + 4c) \times (a + c)$

Casting-out-nines

Verify the following results using Casting-out-nines.

a) $112065 + 360085 + 289872 + 156345 = 918367$

b) $4998 + 6789 + 5715 + 4837 + 8976 = 31315$

c) $7534 + 2459 + 1932 + 6547 = 16472$

d) $37467 + 35647 + 285 + 10085 = 82876$

e) $3746735 - 2837546 = 909189$

f) $876542 - 32548 - 698547 = 145447$

g) $658723 + 154639 - 369847 + 367 = 443882$

h) $588 \times 512 = 301056$

i) $842 \times 858 = 722536$

j) $966 \times 973 = 939918$

k) $13579 \div 975, Q = 13, R = 904$

l) $7238761 \div 524, Q = 13184, R = 225$

m) $11199171 \div 99979, Q = 112, R = 1523$

n) $87265 \times 32117 = 2802690005$

o) $6471 \times 6212 = 40197852$

p) $(207)^2 = 42849$
q) $(2134)^2 = 4553856$
r) $(3247)^2 = 10542169$
s) $(12)^3 = 1729$
t) $(65)^3 = 98002$

Factorization of cubic polynomials

a) $x^3 + 13x^2 + 31x - 45$
b) $x^3 - 2x^2 - x + 2$
c) $x^3 - 3x^2 - 9x - 5$
d) $y^3 - 2y^2 - 29y - 42$
e) $x^3 - 10x^2 - 53x - 42$
f) $x^3 - 23x^2 + 142x - 120$
g) $y^3 - 7y + 6$
h) $x^3 + 9x^2 + 24x + 16$
i) $x^3 + 10x^2 + 27x + 18$

Linear equations

Solve the following:
a) $9x + 9 = 7x + 7$

b) $\dfrac{1}{x - 8} + \dfrac{1}{x - 9} = \dfrac{1}{x - 5} + \dfrac{1}{x - 12}$

c) $\dfrac{1}{x - 1} + \dfrac{1}{x - 3} = \dfrac{1}{x - 4} + \dfrac{1}{x - 8}$

d) $\dfrac{3}{3x - 1} - \dfrac{6}{6x - 1} = \dfrac{3}{3x - 2} - \dfrac{2}{2x - 1}$

e) $\dfrac{(x + 3)^3}{(x + 5)^3} = \dfrac{x + 1}{x + 7}$

Quadratic equations

Solve the following quadratic equations.
a) $(x - 2/x + 2)^2 + 6 = 5 (x - 2/x + 2)$
b) $(7x - 1/x)^2 + 3(7x - 1/x) = 18$
c) $6(y - 3/2y + 1) + 1 = 5(y - 3/2y + 1)^2$
d) $1/x - 4 - 1/x - 7 = 11/30$
e) $x/x + 1 + x + 1/x = 13/6$
f) $3/x - 1 - 1/x - 2 - 1/x - 3 = 0$
g) $2x - 3/x - 1 - 4(x - 1/2x - 3) = 3$
h) $x/x + 1 + x + 1/x = 25/12$
i) $2x + 3/x + 4(x/2x + 3) = 13/3$
j) $(2x + 1) + 3/2x + 1 = 4$

Harder factor

1. $3x^2 + xy - 2y^2 - 4xy - yz - zx$
2. $2x^2 + 2y^2 + 5xy + 2x - 5y - 12$
3. $6x^2 - 8y^2 - 6z^2 + 2xy + 16yz + 5xz$
4. $x^2 + 3y^2 + 2z^2 + 4xy + 3xz + 7yz$
5. $3x^2 + 7xy + 2y^2 + 11xz + 7yz + 6z^2 + 14x + 8y + 14z + 8$

Simultaneous equations

Solve for x and y:
a) $23x + 29y = 42; 46x + 14y = 84$
b) $7y - 2x = 5; 8y + 7x = 15$
c) $30u + 44v = 10; 40u + 55v = 13$
d) $152x - 378y = -74; -378x + 152y = -604$
e) $x + 3y = 6; 2x - 3y = 12$

f) $x + y = 9$; $8x - y = 0$

g) $217x + 131y = 913$; $131x + 217y = 827$

h) $2x + 5y = 13$; $2x + 3y = 4$

i) $5x + 3y = 19xy$; $7x - 2x = 8xy$

j) $x + y = 63$; $3x - 4y = 0$

Multiplication

Multiply the following and check the results using the Casting-out-nines method.

a) 36×34

b) 87×83

c) 128×122

d) 112×998

e) 688×988

f) 107×95

g) 9997×9998

h) 252×248

i) 148×149

j) 506×494

k) 2487×9999

l) 87904×99999

m) 8284×99

n) 43427×9999

o) 144×9999

p) 279×331

q) 7628×4287

r) 144×66

Trigonometry

a) If $\sin A = 8/17$, find the value of the other five trigonometric ratios

b) If $\tan A = 9/40$, find the value of $\sin 2A$, $\cos 2A$, $\tan 2A$ and $\sec 2A$

c) If $\cos A = 3/5$, find the value of $\sin 3A$, $\cos 3A$ and $\tan 3A$

d) If $\sin A = 8/10$, find the value of $\sin A/2$, $\cos A/2$ and $\tan A/2$

e) If $\sin A = 3/5$, $\sin B = 8/17$ find $\sin(A + B)$, $\cos(A + B)$

f) If $\sin A = 12/13$, $\sin B = 8/17$ find $\sin(A - B)$, $\cos(A - B)$

Integration

Integrate the following using the Vedic formula.

1. $\int x.\sin x \, dx$ 2. $\int x.\sin 3x \, dx$ 3. $\int x^2 e^x \, dx$

4. $\int x.\log x \, dx$ 5. $\int x.\sec^2 x \, dx$ 6. $\int \dfrac{3x-1}{(x-1)\,(x-2)\,(x-3)} dx$

7. $\int \dfrac{2x \, dx}{x^2 + 3x+2}$ 8. $\int \dfrac{x}{(x+2)\,(x-1)^3} dx$

Determinants

Solve the following.

1. $\begin{vmatrix} 2 & 4 \\ -5 & -1 \end{vmatrix}$ 2. $\begin{vmatrix} 2 & 7 & 65 \\ 3 & 8 & 75 \\ 5 & 9 & 85 \end{vmatrix}$ 3. $\begin{vmatrix} 1 & 1 & 2 \\ 2 & 1 & -3 \\ 5 & 4 & -9 \end{vmatrix}$

4. $\begin{vmatrix} 3 & -1 & -2 \\ 0 & 0 & -1 \\ 3 & -5 & 0 \end{vmatrix}$ 5. $\begin{vmatrix} 3 & -4 & 5 \\ 1 & 1 & -2 \\ 2 & 3 & 1 \end{vmatrix}$

Coordinate geometry

1. Find the equation of a line passing through (1, 2) and (3, 6).
2. Find the equation of line passing through (3,1) and (9, 1).
3. Find the distance between
   a) (2, 3) and (4, 1)   b) (−5, −7) and (−1, 3)

4. Determine the ratio in which the line $2x + y = 4$ divides the line segment joining the point A(2, – 2) and B(3, 7)

5. Find the ratio in which the line segment joins the points (– 3, 10) and (6, – 8) is divided by the point (– 1, 6).

Answers

HCF of polynomials

a) $3(m - 2)$
b) $a(a + 3)$
c) $m + 4$
d) $x - 5$
e) $2(x^2 + 1)$

Differentiation

a) $-x^2 \sin x + 2x\cos x$
b) $-3\sin^4 x \cos^2 x + 3\cos^4 x \sin^2 x$
c) $(3x + 5)\sec^2 x + 3(1 + \tan x)$
d) $2\sec^2 x \tan x$
e) $4(12x + 7)(6x^2 + 7x)^3$
f) $2(3 + \sec^2(x))\cos(3x + \tan(x))$
g) $f'(x) = 20x^3 - 9x^2 + 14x - 9$
   $f''(x) = f^{(2)}(x) = 60x^2 + 18x + 14$
   $f''(x) = f^{(3)}(x) = 120x - 18$
h) $y' = 2\sin x\cos x$
   $y'' = 2\cos^2 x - 2\sin^2 x$
   $y''' = -8\sin x\cos x$

Division of polynomials

1. $3x + 5$
2. $x^2 + x - 6$
3. $2y^2 + 4y + 8$
4. $x^2 + 4x + 4$
5. $a^2 - 2a + 4$
6. $4m - 3$

Combined operations

1. 222387
2. 81192
3. 2599
4. 10378
5. 9274
6. 52

Cubes

a) 941192	b) 12167	c) 74088
d) 1225043	e) 976191488	f) 1953125
g) 9800344		

Squares

a) 180625	b) 10804369	c) 361
d) 84681	e) 12769	f) 988036
g) 1369	h) 113569	

Multiplication of polynomials

i) $8x^2 + 26xy + 21y^2$
j) $2a^2 + 25az + 77z^2$
k) $9x^4 + 43x^2z + 28z^2$
d) $2x^4 + 18x^3 + 17x^2 + 13x - 63$
l) $20x^4 - 71x^3 + 71x^2 - 135x - 64$
m) $7x^4 + 27x^3 + 46x^2 - 24x$
n) $36x^3 + 27x^2 - 28x$
o) $56x^4 + 16x^3 + 68x^2 + 8x + 26$
p) $8x^2 + 38xy + 42x^2$
q) $2a^2 + 6ac + 4c^2$

Casting-out-nines

a) Correct   b) Correct   c) Incorrect   d) Incorrect
e) Correct   f) Correct   g) Correct   h) Correct
i) Incorrect   j) Correct   k) Correct   l) Incorrect
m) Correct   n) Correct   o) Correct   p) Correct
q) Incorrect   r) Incorrect

Factors of cubic polynomials

a) $(x - 1) (x + 5) (x + 9)$
b) $(x - 2) (x - 1) (x + 1)$
c) $(x - 1) (x + 1)(x - 5)$
d) $(y + 2) (y + 3) (y - 7)$
e) $(x + 1) (x + 3) (x - 14)$
f) $(x - 1) (x - 10) (x - 12)$
g) $(y - 1) (y + 3) (y - 2)$
h) $(x + 4) (x + 4) (x + 1)$
i) $(x + 2) (x + 5) (x + 1)$

Linear equations

1. $x = -1$ 2. $x = 8\frac{1}{2}$ 3. $x = 3\frac{1}{2}$
4. $x = -5/12$ 5. $x = -4$

Quadratic equations

a) $x = -6, -4$
b) $x = 1/4, 1/13$
c) $x = 4, 13/2$
d) $x = 3, -1/2$
e) $x = 2; y = -3$
f) $x = 4 \pm \sqrt{3}$
g) $x = 1/2, 4/3$
h) $x = 3, -4$
i) $x = 3, -9/2$
j) $x = 0, 1$

Harder factor

1. $(x - y - z)(3x - y + 2z)$
2. $(x + 2y + 3)(2x - y - 4)$
3. $(2x - 2y + 3z)(3x + 4y - 2z)$
4. $(x + y + 2z)(x + 3y + z)$
5. $(x + 2y + 3z + 4)(3x + y + 2z + 2)$

Simultaneous equations

a) $x = 42/13; y = 0$
b) $x = 1; y = 1$
c) $u = 1/5; v = 1/4$

d) x = 2; y = 1
e) x = 6; y = 0
f) x = 1; y = 8
g) x = 3; y = 2
h) x = − 19/4; y = 9/2
i   x = 1/3; y = 1/2
j)   x = 36; y = 27

Multiplication

a) 1224   b) 7221   c) 15616   d) 111776
e) 679744 f) 10165   g) 99950006 h) 62496
i) 22052   j) 249964 k) 24867513 l) 8790372096
m) 820116 n) 424226573 o) 1439856 p) 92349
q) 2701236 r) 13824

Trigonometry

a) cos A = 15/17, tan A = 8/15
b) sin 2A = 720/1681, cos 2A = 1519/1681; tan 2A = 720/1519
c) sin 3A = 236/125; cos 3A = − 117/125; tan 3A = −236/117
d) sin A/2 = $\sqrt{2}$ /$\sqrt{5}$; cos A/2 = 2/$\sqrt{5}$; tan A/2 = 1/$\sqrt{2}$
e) sin(A + B) = 77/85; cos(A + B) = 36/85
f) sin(A − B) = 140/221; cos(A − B) = 171/221

Integration

1. − x cos x + sin x + c
2. − 1/3cos3x + 1/9sin 3x +c
3. ex (x^2 − 2x + 2) + c

4. $1/2 \ x^2 \log x - 1/4 \ x^2 + c$
5. $x.\tan x - \log \cos x + c$
6. $\log(x - 1) - 5\log(x - 2) + 4\log(x - 3) + c$
7. $4\log(x + 2) - 2\log(x + 1) + c$

8. $2/9 \ \{\log(x - 1) - \log(x + 2)\} - \dfrac{1}{3(x-1)} + c$

Determinants

1. 18   2. 0   3. 0   4. -12 5. 46

Co-ordinate geometry

1. $y = 2x$ 2) $x = 3y$ 3) $2\sqrt{2}$ unit
4) $4\sqrt{2}$ unit   5) 2:9   6) 2:7